THE HEARTWOOD BEACH

A HEARTWOOD SISTERS NOVEL (CARTER'S COVE BOOK 3)

ELANA JOHNSON

ISBN-13: 978-1953506269

1

Sheryl Heartwood checked through the peephole to find her best friends standing on her front porch. She unlocked the door and removed the chain before stepping back to face Abby and Tyler Bryan.

"Hey, guys," she said, glancing behind them to find that truck still parked right on the edge of her property.

Ricky Van Nuy had been following her home for a couple of weeks now, and she seriously couldn't sleep in this house for another night with that truck there. In an instance like this, she wished she lived with one of her sisters, the way Gwen and Celeste did. Or the hotel like Olympia. Alissa lived too far away from civilization, and she couldn't imagine what it would be like to not have someone close enough to hear her scream.

She couldn't see Ricky as her friends came in, their little chowchow on a leash, waddling in after them. "I just need to pull the pizza out of the oven," she said. Sheryl didn't cook often, and she rarely turned on the oven in the summertime. But she'd needed a reason to get her friends over here.

"Smells good," Tyler said, bending to unclip the leash on All-Star's collar. "You said you had a problem. Something to do with that truck parked out front?"

"Yes," Sheryl said. "How did you know?"

"There was a guy there when we pulled up," Abby said, pulling out a barstool and sitting down while Sheryl opened a bag of Caesar salad. "But he ducked down when we got out of the car."

So Ricky was out there. Sheryl's heartbeat bobbed around in the back of her throat. She cleared the emotion away and turned to get the pizza out of the oven as the timer went off. "My sister said I should hire someone to be my bodyguard. I was hoping you guys would know someone."

Sheryl worked at her family's hotel, resort, and spa, and her hours taking care of the grounds started well before dawn. Ricky hadn't been bothering her before work. Only after. She wasn't sure when Ricky left at night, because she refused to sit by the window and watch his truck.

"I'm sure we can find someone," Tyler said. "Doesn't Pops work at The Heartwood Inn?" he asked his wife.

"Pops works the swing shift," Abby said. "Sheryl's done early in the day, right?"

"Usually by two," Sheryl said. It was too hot to do much after that, and she and her crew put in eight hours every day long before two o'clock came. She loved her schedule, as she could take a quick cat nap and then be rested for the summer evening activities on the island.

She loved Carter's Cove and the nighttime energy that existed during the summer months. Some people found the tourists annoying, but Sheryl loved the surfing competition, the bonfire, the tennis and golf tournaments, the dog championship, the classic car parade, all of it.

But the thought of being out in public past dark had terrified her these past few days, and she'd missed a few things.

The bonfire was in two nights, and she was *not* going to miss it. Ricky was not going to keep her inside, behind locked and chained doors. Oh, no, he was not.

"I know a guy," Tyler said. "But he has another job in the mornings."

"I don't need him in the mornings," Sheryl said. "Just the afternoons and evenings. I can pay him to hang out with me." She hated the way that sounded, but she had a legitimate reason this time.

Not that she'd hired a man to spend time with her before. Sheryl wasn't desperate, and she hadn't minded being a third wheel for her friends as one by one, they all found a man and got married.

Sheryl hadn't really minded—until she didn't have

anyone to come sleep on her couch and make sure she was safe at night.

"His name is Gage Sanders," Tyler said. "He's ex-military, and he works security at the ferry in the mornings until at least noon."

"Maybe he won't have time," Abby said. "You should text him."

Tyler held up his phone. "I just did." He reached for a plate and took a couple pieces of pizza. He held up one and grinned. "I think he'll do it. Gage doesn't have a lot going on in the afternoons, if you know what I mean."

A few seconds passed before Sheryl got what he meant. "It's not a date," she said, rolling her eyes.

"Why not?" Abby asked.

"Why not?" Sheryl asked, her voice pitching up. "I'm not interested in dating."

"But why not?" Abby scooped some salad onto her plate, only glancing at Sheryl as if she didn't get why Sheryl didn't want to involve a man in her life again. She wasn't even sure she had all the pieces of her heart back from the last time she'd tried a relationship.

Chuck Goldsmith had left Carter's Cove, and he'd taken Sheryl's heart with him. It might have been a year or two—maybe three—but Sheryl had learned to find joy in her work, and she still had friends who invited her to do things with them.

Sometimes.

Tyler's phone chimed, and he practically lunged for it. "It's Gage."

Sheryl pretended like she didn't care as she dug around in the lettuce for a crouton.

"What did he say?" Abby finally asked, swatting at Tyler. "You're killing us."

Tyler just grinned his goofy smile and swiped his blond hair out of his eyes. He looked a little like a surfer, though he ran a digital marketing company for the small businesses on the island.

Sheryl unconsciously reached up and patted her own blonde hair, her scalp suddenly aching from how she kept her hair in a perpetual ponytail. She pulled her hairband out, her own curiosity reaching epic proportions.

"He said he's been thinking about getting another gig in the afternoon," Tyler said as if he were reading from the screen of his phone. "He said he's interested."

Interested.

Sheryl reminded herself he wasn't interested in *her*. He was interested in the job.

"He wants to set something up," Tyler said. "Should I give him your number, or do you want his?"

"Give me his," Sheryl said. A moment later, her phone buzzed, and Tyler had forwarded the contact. "I'm going to text him right now." She did, and Gage responded immediately with *I can come over tonight.*

Sheryl almost choked, and Abby heard and saw everything. "What?" she asked.

"He wants to come tonight."

"Great," Tyler said. "You need someone right away, right?" He took another big bite of his pizza.

Sheryl didn't know what to say. She didn't want Gage to come over while her friends were here. Or did she?

"Let's go," Abby said, though she hadn't finished eating.

Tyler looked back and forth between the two women. "I'm missing something."

"Nope," Abby said, popping the P. "Sheryl needs privacy for her job interview. We can take our food with us."

"Take it," Sheryl said, glancing down at her phone. She quickly typed out, *Sure thing*, and added her address to the text before sending it.

Everything happened so fast after that. Abby and Tyler left, and Sheryl chained herself back in her house, the truck on the street inspiring more fear in her than she knew what to do with.

Gage had said he'd "be there soon," but it felt like a long time until he pulled into her driveway on a sleek, shiny, black motorcycle. Sheryl's view through the slats in the blinds was limited, but wow. Gage had long legs, and as he stood from his bike, he sported a broad pair of shoulders in a sexy, leather jacket.

He pulled off his helmet and didn't look around, his confidence oozing off of him and hitting her in the chest, even through the glass.

He had dark hair and a rugged, handsome face that had her breath catching in the back of her throat. She watched him walk up the sidewalk and onto her porch. Still, when he knocked, she flinched.

"Get ahold of yourself," she muttered as she scampered away from the window and tugged on the bottom of her shirt. Looking down, horror washed through her when she realized she hadn't even changed out of her gardening clothes. Mud dotted her jeans from a repotting project earlier that day.

The kitchen was a mess too, and the scent of pizza hung in the air. Sheryl didn't want to open the door, and she stepped over to the blinds again. Maybe she could just text him that she'd made a mistake. Didn't need his private security services.

He knocked again, this time calling, "Sheryl, is everything okay in there?"

To her complete horror, Ricky got out of his truck and approached her house. For some reason, that had her sprinting over to the door. Her fingers fumbled on the chain and slipped on the lock, but she got the door open.

Gage stood there, half turned toward her and half watching Ricky cross the lawn. Ricky froze too, and Sheryl felt like she'd been dropped inside a movie where something was about to blow up. Everything moved in slow motion, but she managed to say, "Gage, hey," in a casual, easy voice that betrayed everything she felt inside.

He turned back toward her, questions in those dark, dreamy, dangerous eyes.

"Who is this guy?" Ricky called to her, and Sheryl wanted the ground to open up and swallow him whole. He'd never approached the house before, and she'd had people over. Never a single man who rode a sexy motorcycle, but still.

"Kiss me," she hissed, and surprise shot across Gage's expression. Panic built inside her with every passing second, and she was sure the gorgeous man on her porch would scowl, stomp away, and leave her there with Ricky.

She stepped out onto the porch at the same time Gage's arm slipped around her waist. "You need to leave," she called to Ricky.

"Who is he?" Ricky asked again.

Before Sheryl could call to him that Gage was her boyfriend, he held her close, leaned down, and looked right into her eyes. "This isn't a joke, right? He's your problem?"

Oh, Sheryl had problems, but at that particular moment she couldn't remember them.

She didn't recall speaking. Acknowledging Gage's question in any way. He must've been able to read minds or see something in her eyes, because he brought his mouth to hers and kissed her like she'd never been kissed before.

2

*G*age couldn't believe he'd gone along with this plan. Or how much he enjoyed kissing the blonde woman he'd literally met thirty seconds ago. But her lips were soft, and she melted right into his arms the way his previous girlfriends had.

She's not your girlfriend, his mind screamed, and it was loud enough to make him pull back. He cleared his throat and looked over his shoulder to see the other man still standing there, staring.

"You should go," he said, employing his Marine voice and hoping that would be enough to get this guy off her front lawn.

"Go, Ricky," Sheryl said, and Gage kept his body mostly in front of her.

Ricky's fists clenched, but he didn't take another step

forward. A moment later, he spun and stomped back to his truck, where he got in and drove off.

Sheryl's relief filled the air, and Gage stepped away from her as the small truck rounded the corner with screeching wheels. His body temperature felt off-the-charts, but that could've been the summer evening heat.

In fact, it *had* to be the summer evening heat, because he was not interested in another blonde fiasco.

"Thank you," she said, stepping back into her house. "Do you want to come in?"

He wasn't sure he should, as he felt like all the steps were out of order now. He wasn't even sure he'd have noticed this woman on the ferry if he'd seen her. She was pretty, with a clear pair of blue eyes that flitted all over the place as if she couldn't look directly at him. Her blonde hair hung down to her shoulders, and it looked like it could use a hairbrush. He didn't mind so much, as he'd felt it between his fingers, and it was silky smooth.

"I have pizza here," she said from somewhere inside, and Gage practically jumped into her house so she wouldn't realize he'd been standing on the porch like a doofus.

You need the job, he told himself as he closed the door behind him. And she obviously needed his help. He glanced around her house, almost hating himself for how he assessed which windows he could go out, and how he looked up to the ceiling as if a trained assassin would be clinging to the fan there.

But he'd spent two decades in the Marines, and he'd been trained to see things other people didn't even know to look for. Sheryl had no intruders in her living room. In fact, she had blue and yellow curtains on the windows, matching pillows on the couch, and plenty of pizza still sitting on her kitchen counter.

Gage had already eaten dinner, but he'd never say no to pizza. He joined her in the kitchen at the back of the house, where she had real cloth napkins next to the paper plates. They seemed at odds with one another, but he didn't comment on it.

"So you can obviously see why I need your services," she said, her voice cool and detached. "That man is Ricky Van Nuy. He used to work for me at the inn."

"The inn?"

"Oh, my sisters and I all work at our family's inn. The Heartwood Inn?" She looked at him then, her eyebrows raised.

Gage knew The Heartwood Inn, that was for sure. It was the premier resort and hotel on the island, with the largest private beach with huge summer events that brought thousands of people to the island of Carter's Cove.

He could do without the tourists, but without them, he wouldn't have a way to pay his bills. And as it was, standing on the ferry or the docks on either end of the ferry route wearing a pair of CIA shades and a tight, black shirt was barely making ends meet.

Jim gave him as much work as possible, and he'd been working for the local police department as security at some of the bigger island events. He'd been on-duty at the dog championship, and he'd just signed on to walk the crowd in uniform with a badge for the huge surfing championship at Sheryl's beach in just about a week or so.

"Anyway," Sheryl said, clearing her throat.

Gage realized he hadn't answered her.

"I just need—"

"I know The Heartwood Inn," he blurted out, interrupting her. Their eyes met, and she looked more afraid of him than the Ricky dude on the front lawn. "I grew up in a town outside of Savannah, and we came to Carter's Cove several times."

"Oh, maybe you stayed at our inn."

"No," he said, wondering who she thought he was. "We couldn't afford The Heartwood." He realized too late how his words sounded. Plus, he'd had a girlfriend or two—or three or four—that had told him sometimes his speaking voice sounded like a bark.

"Oh." Sheryl blinked, the shock plain to see on her face. She turned away from him, almost hesitantly, as if she wanted to keep one eye on him but not look at him at the same time. "Did you want something to drink? Salad?"

"The pizza's fine," he said, picking up a piece of cold pizza. He didn't care. He loved pizza in all its forms, and he asked, "Have you been to Pie Squared?"

"The new place by the ferry?"

"Yeah."

"I've been by," she said evasively.

"Which means no," he said, trying to put a smile on his face. It honestly felt like a scowl, and he wiped it away quickly. Which meant Sheryl didn't see it by the time she turned around.

"I haven't been down that way since they opened," she said.

Of course she hadn't. She lived in a quaint, quiet neighborhood bordering the beach. Everything about her house, the street it was on, and the clothes she wore screamed of sophistication and wealth, two things Gage didn't have much experience with.

Sure, her jeans were muddy, but they still cost more than he'd ever paid for an article of clothing. The only thing he'd ever put any money into was his motorcycle, and he simply wanted to be on the bike right now, riding away from her.

"I need someone to pick me up at work," she said. "I get off at two, but I can hang around the hotel to accommodate your schedule."

He nodded and took another bite of his pizza. She continued with, "I just need to get home safely. Then you can go. Maybe come back in the evening to make sure Ricky isn't here bothering me. It shouldn't take up too much of your time."

"Time I have, sweetheart," he said.

She frowned at him, and he catalogued the fact that she

didn't like his nickname. Fair enough. It was a little demeaning, and he held up his hands as if surrendering. "Sorry. I'm sorry. But I have time. I have a few jobs I do for the city, but we can go over that if you think you want to hire me."

He cursed himself for being such a jerk. "I'm a nice guy, really."

She nodded and ran her hand over her hair as if to smooth it back. Her hand moved to tuck her hair, and Gage appreciated her beauty in that moment. He finished his pizza, and said, "Okay, I'll go and let you decide. You have my number."

Shaking his head as his thoughts started berating him, he walked back toward the front door.

"You didn't ask how much the pay was," she said behind him.

He paused and turned back. "How much?"

"You tell me, Mister Sanders. I'm unfamiliar with hiring people to make sure I get home safe."

"Oh, honey," he said, unable to help himself. "I'm not just a person. I'm a man. A Marine. And if you hire me, Ricky will never bother you again." He opened the door but didn't step through it. "You decide what you need, and we'll talk price."

"But what would you charge?" she asked, her footsteps hurrying toward him as he stepped onto the porch. He took his shades out of his breast pocket and situated them on his face. It really was beautiful here, and he didn't want to go back to Peach Tree. Or the city. Or Whistlestop Shores.

No, he liked Carter's Cove, and he just needed to figure out a way to have enough work to stay here.

"Twenty per hour," he said. "You decide how many hours you need me. Put together a sample schedule, that kind of thing, and we'll talk again." He went down her steps without looking back, because while he wanted the job, he didn't want her to know he wanted the job.

He climbed on his bike and started her up, the loud roar of the engine filling this tranquil neighborhood. With his eyes hiding behind the mirrored shades, he could watch Sheryl, and even from a distance, he saw the distaste roll across her face.

Gage grinned as he backed out of her driveway and gunned his bike down the road. He honestly wasn't a jerk, but he was who he was, and she should know it before she hired him. He drove around the island a bit, getting away from the larger crowds, which mostly stuck to the downtown area.

He stopped by the grocery store and bought apples and pears to make a tart, and he put together a delicious dessert. Through it all, he couldn't stop thinking about that kiss on that porch with that blonde woman.

"What do you think?" he asked his dog, who lay right on the line he'd established for her, just outside the kitchen. Britta didn't answer, of course, and he tossed her a small chunk of hot dog and went back to cleaning up while the tart baked.

And thinking about Sheryl.

"Enough," he told himself as the timer went off and he pulled his tart out of the oven. It was perfect—and he didn't want to eat a bite of it.

His first thought was to take it to Sheryl and apologize, ask her to please hire him, and he'd see her at two o'clock the next day. Instead, he left it to cool on the counter, and he went down the hall in his much more run-down beach cottage to go to bed.

After all, being on the ferry by six a.m. came pretty early in the morning.

"Morning," he said to Walker Hardwicke as Gage stepped from land to ferry. He rode with Walker almost every day, rain or shine. The man never deviated from much of anything, and this morning was no different. He wore a Florida Falcons hat to cover his bald head, a pair of sunglasses though it certainly wasn't too bright yet, and he wore a pair of black shorts with a white shirt that had the ferry logo on the chest.

"Morning," he said, the clipboard in his hand already. He moved around and checked things off while Gage yawned. He worked the ferry system until one, which left him enough time to run home and make a sandwich for lunch before grabbing the tart and heading further inland to The Heartwood Inn.

Sheryl, shockingly, had not called or texted him last night. He'd probably scared her too much. Or offended her. Neither of which he actually wanted to do. Sometimes, he was just rough around the edges. Being raised by a single mother and following his pops into the military had done that to him.

His last ex-girlfriend's words echoed through his mind. *You can usually get more with sugar than vinegar.*

So he'd get this shift over with, get his tart, and see if he couldn't sweeten Sheryl Heartwood on the idea of hiring him.

3

Sheryl admired the new bark as she pushed and swirled it around in the bed that bordered the scenic walkway between the swimming pools and the tennis courts. This wasn't the most-used path, but it deserved to be beautiful too, for anyone who chose to come down this way.

She exhaled as she stood up, dusting her hands on her pants though she wore gloves. She loved getting her nails done, and the gloves were essentially to ensure she wasn't just throwing money away at the salon.

Her back pulled, and sweat beaded on her forehead and the back of her neck. She wiped her face, sure she'd just scraped bark across the bridge of her nose. She didn't care. She just needed to get cleaned up and get back to the office where she ended every one of her shifts. She had paperwork to do, and schedules to attend to, and supplies to order.

She'd brought out a golf cart with a small wagon hitched to it, and she started gathering up her tools and trash. She'd spread sixteen bags of bark in the past couple of hours, and she pulled the golf cart to the last spot where she needed to pick up the empty bags. It was in the dipped curve of the sidewalk, and she literally felt like the only person on the grounds in that moment.

A sound clicked behind her, almost like the chain on a bicycle, and she turned to see who was coming so she could get out of the way.

The sidewalk remained empty. The branches of the tree farthest from her waved, but the air was absolutely still. No wind. Not even a breeze coming off the ocean. If she were down on the beach, there would at least be a whiff of a breeze.

Her skin crawled, and her heart started to pound in the back of her throat. She swiped the empty bags from the beds she'd barked and mashed them in her hands. She'd been thinking about Gage a lot since he'd roared off on that sexy, sleek, scary motorcycle.

That kiss.

Those hands.

The bike.

The man had a lot to admire, but he wasn't really her type. At all. Not even a little bit. She didn't like being talked down to, and she didn't like the peace on her street being disrupted by a loud motorcycle.

Of course, the peace on her street had been disrupted with the appearance of Ricky's truck parked outside her place. And now she was fairly certain he was just down the path, watching her.

She felt his eyes on her, and her fingers started to shake. Punching down the bags, she hurried to get behind the wheel of the golf cart. She'd sat down when she heard that clicking again, and she couldn't help turning to look over her shoulder.

Sure enough, Ricky stood there, his hands on the handlebars of a bike and a dark look on his face.

"Leave me alone," she called to him. She started the golf cart and jammed her foot on the accelerator, telling herself not to look back. *Don't look back. Don't look back.*

She made it back to the groundskeeping shed, but Ricky knew where that was. He could simply ride his bike on over. Thankfully, Barry was there.

"Hey," she said. "Can you clean this up for me? I have a conference call with my sister I need to get to."

"Sure thing," he said, still winding up a hose he'd been using. He flashed her a smile, but Sheryl couldn't return it. She hurried into her office, intending to close and lock the door behind her. She'd hide out here for a little bit, then go up to the restaurant and get a late lunch. She could hang by the pool until Celeste left the hotel. Maybe she could sleep at her sisters' place tonight too. Gwen and Celeste shared a house, and they had a spare bedroom.

"There you are," a man said, and Sheryl screamed, her arms flailing out in front of her as she turned back toward the hallway she'd just entered from.

The man there grunted, and her hands met something hard and metallic just before whatever he held hit the floor.

"It's me," Gage said over her screaming. "Gage."

She cut off the shriek ripping her throat and stared at him. Their eyes met, and he certainly didn't look happy. His gaze dropped to the floor, and Sheryl followed his lead.

"Is that a...pie?"

"It was a tart, actually," he said. "I made it for you to help this apology go more smoothly."

Something clanged behind him, and Sheryl's panic reared again. "Just come in," she said, grabbing onto his elbow and hefting him into her office. She slammed the door behind him and locked it.

A sigh slipped from her lips, and she carefully avoided the splattered fruit on the floor as she moved over to her desk. There was barely enough room for the two of them, plus the mess on the ground, and Sheryl stumbled into her chair.

"You seem on-edge," Gage said.

"I am on-edge," she said acidly. "You would be too if

someone was stalking you." She gave him a dirty look. "What are you doing here?"

"I came to apologize," he said, knocking on her desk as she didn't have another chair in her office. She didn't need one, as no one came in here with her. "And I was hoping you'd offer me the job."

Sheryl scoffed, though she didn't have anyone else for the position, and the thought of going home alone was absolutely terrifying. Wasn't happening. She didn't want to involve her sisters more than she already had, and Celeste would ask a thousand questions—and not only about the stalker.

"Okay," Gage said, his voice a little too high. "I'm sorry about the tart. It was actually really good. I think you would've liked it." He stepped over to the door and unlocked it.

"What kind was it?" she asked.

"Apple and pear."

"Where did you get it?"

He stooped to pick up the pan, and Sheryl turned to get a roll of paper towels from the closet behind her. She crouched to help him as he said, "I didn't get it anywhere. I made it."

"You made it?" She stalled in the scooping of pie filling into the pan he held. "Like...you baked it?"

"That's right." His dark eyes sparkled, and Sheryl thought she could probably get lost in eyes like that. You know, if she even liked this guy, which she did not.

"When?"

"Last night."

"How long does it take to make a tart like this?" He'd left her house about eight, and she knew he worked early at the ferry.

"I don't sleep much," he admitted.

In that moment, he became real, and Sheryl ducked her head and she continued to clean up. With all the filling off the floor and in the pan, he straightened. The mood between them sent beats of awkwardness into the air, and Sheryl wiped her hands as Gage clearly stalled at the door.

"I need you," she finally blurted. "I don't want to stay here and waste time, and I can't go home by myself."

Gage considered her, those dark eyes seeing so much more than she wanted him to. "Twenty dollars an hour?"

"Yes," she said. "And I want you to come home with me and stay for dinner." Her nerves fired through her system. "I want to take a nap, and you can chill on the couch or something. I have a cat, but she won't come out."

He simply looked at her, and she had no idea what he was thinking. He wore a perfect mask, and it was almost unnerving. "I have a dog I need to swing by and get, if you don't mind."

"I don't mind. I love dogs," she said, her heart taking courage. "So you'll do it?"

"What's the job description, exactly?" he asked. "I feel like we need to go over specifics."

"I don't want to be alone," Sheryl said, thinking that summed things up pretty nicely. "I don't want to be afraid at work. Or on the way home from work. Or at home." Her throat was so dry, but she continued anyway. "I want to go to the fun events on the island this summer, but I can't, because I can't come back to my house alone, in the dark."

She swallowed and met his eyes. Sympathy swirled in his eyes, as well as a definite edge of darkness. Oh, yes, Gage Sanders was not to be trifled with, and Sheryl really liked that he was big and strong and capable of protecting her.

"So you want me to show up here at two, and take you home, and then do whatever you're doing or whatever you want to do."

"About that, yeah," she said, her voice on the edge of a quiver. She hated that she'd allowed Ricky to unsettle her so much.

"All right," he said. "If I can bring my dog along for some things, I'm in."

"No problem," Sheryl said. She reached for her purse. "Did you drive? Or do you have a helmet for your dog?"

SHERYL SAT ON HER BACK STEPS, SMILING AS GAGE THREW A ball for his dog. The mutt could only find it in the sand every other time, but she sure seemed to be having fun.

Sheryl had originally thought she'd take a nap, but she hadn't been able to fall asleep with Gage in her house.

So she'd gotten up to find him dozing on the couch, his dog all wrapped up in his legs. It reminded her that Gage was human—until he'd spoken with his eyes still closed. "I know you're there," he'd said.

"I can't sleep," she'd said. "Let's go out to the beach."

He'd gotten up while she made lemonade, and now she sat in the shade while Britta rooted around in the sand for the ball she couldn't find. Gage ended up collecting it for her, and they came back to the deck.

"Phew," Gage said as he sank down. "It's hot today." He picked up his glass of lemonade and took a long drink. "What's on the summer calendar tonight?" he asked.

"I think it's the hot dog roast," she said, her distaste obvious in her tone.

"And we don't like hot dogs?"

"It's all teenagers and singles," she said.

"Are you not single?" he asked, glancing at her.

Heat filled her, making her face feel like it had burst into flames. "I am," she said. "But the hot dog roast is for singles in their early twenties. Not for us."

He chuckled even as he nodded. "How old do you think I am?"

"Um." She didn't need to embarrass herself. "I know you served in the Marines for a long time."

"Two decades."

"And that you retired recently."

He looked at her expectantly.

"Forty?"

"Close," he said. "Thirty-nine."

"Guess my age," she said, shaking her head so her hair fanned out around her face. She ducked her head and looked up at him through her eyelashes.

He laughed, and Sheryl didn't know the man was capable of such a sound. "Oh, I'm not playing that game," he said. "I'm smarter than you think I am."

"Fine," she said. "But I'm a decade too old for the hot dog roast, if that tells you anything."

"What about the bonfire?" he asked, and if Sheryl didn't know better, she'd say he was flirting with her.

Flirting.

Impossible. Gage Sanders didn't know how to flirt.

But he knows how to kiss.

Flames burst along every inch of her skin, and she looked away. "The bonfire is acceptable."

"Great," he said, groaning as he stood. "I think I'm going to go try to make that tart again." He left her sitting on the back steps, utterly confused. He had so many pieces to him, and she was having trouble fitting them all together.

She reached over and patted Britta absently. "He's kind of complicated, isn't he?"

The dog just continued to pant. Sheryl pulled out her

phone and scrolled through her texts until she came to Abby's name.

I need more info on this Gage guy....

4

Gage whistled as he went to work the morning of the bonfire. "Morning," he said to Walker, just like always.

"What are you so happy about?" the man asked, checking something on that clipboard.

"Nothing."

"Right." Walker scoffed. "You've shown up for two mornings in a row, smiling *and* whistling."

"I'm capable of smiling and whistling," Gage said.

"I suspected so," Walker said. "I've just never seen it."

Gage didn't know how to argue with him. It wasn't like he had a lot to smile and whistle about on the ferry. In fact, he was supposed to look imposing and intimidating.

"Erika and I are going to the bonfire tonight," Walker said. "You're welcome to come."

"Oh, I uh...." Gage didn't know what to say. "I'm going

with a client." Of course, the way he'd been thinking about Sheryl wasn't exactly businesslike. He'd spent a couple of afternoons and evenings with her, and it was much better than trying to find something to keep himself and Britta busy in his non-working hours.

No, they hadn't done anything earth-shattering. Time on the beach, then making her a new tart before she whipped up a meal of steak and grilled vegetables. Yesterday, she'd shown him the maritime museum, somewhere he hadn't been on the island yet, though he'd lived here for the past couple of years since he'd retired from the Marines.

Spending time with her was easy. He could talk to her, though they hadn't done much more than share about their families. Fine, Sheryl had done most of that. Gage hadn't said a whole lot about anything.

He didn't exactly have secrets. He just didn't see the point of hashing over things he couldn't change.

A voice inside him that sounded dangerously like his mother told him that he'd have to tell Sheryl something at some point, especially if he wanted to have a relationship with her. But he wasn't sure that was what was happening.

He was her bodyguard, not her boyfriend. Sure, maybe she'd flirted with him a little bit as they worked in her kitchen that first night. Maybe she texted him after he left her house late at night, after Ricky's truck disappeared from the street. Maybe he'd been thinking of the next dessert he could bake and take to her.

And maybe, that night at the bonfire, he could hold her hand. Really find out what she was thinking and if things between them needed to stay strictly professional. His phone buzzed while Walker laughed about "his client."

"What? She really is a client," he said, seeing that Sheryl had texted. She went to work as early as he did, and she'd texted to say, *I'm excited for the bonfire tonight.*

He wasn't sure what that meant. She was excited to go with him? Or just excited in general? And if she hadn't hired him, would she have gone alone?

She'd talked about several friends over the past two days, and Gage didn't want to tell her that his only friends were his boss, a co-worker, and the woman who worked in the bakery at the grocery store.

And now, maybe Sheryl. And he couldn't help thinking that he'd like Sheryl to be more than a friend— and that meant he'd have to start sharing some personal things about himself.

I am too, he sent back before shoving his phone in his back pocket, Walker's all-knowing eyes watching every move.

HAVE FUN ON YOUR DATE. WALKER'S PARTING WORDS TO Gage wouldn't stop rotating through his mind. He didn't want to think of his muscle as a date, but the fact was,

Sheryl Heartwood had hired him to basically accompany her everywhere.

I don't like to be alone.

She didn't seem like a weak woman. Simply spooked, and for good reason. In the two days Gage had picked her up at the inn—about to be three—the Ricky character had been hanging around.

Gage didn't think Sheryl even saw him, though she did scan the parking lot when she left the back of the inn, where the groundskeeping offices were. Ricky was no lightweight when it came to loitering in the shadows, just out of sight. Gage had actually waved to him while he held Sheryl's door open for her.

The other man scowled and ducked behind a bigger truck. Gage followed her home on his motorcycle, satisfied that Ricky had gotten the hint and wouldn't be bothering them that night. Upon parking in her driveway in a spot that was quickly becoming his, he took the backpack he'd brought from his saddlebag.

"What's in that?" Sheryl asked as he went into her carport to go up the steps and into her house.

"Clothes for the bonfire," he said.

"You're not just wearing that?" She scanned him, and dang if Gage didn't feel every inch of her gaze on him.

"The bonfire is a little more upscale than shorts and a T-shirt," he said. "Haven't you been?"

"Of course I've been," she said, clearly annoyed by his

question. "They have a local band every year, and this one time, I was seeing a guitarist in a group."

"Then you know you don't wear shorts and a T-shirt," he said.

"Some people will be," she argued.

Gage suppressed the sigh he wanted to hiss through his teeth. "Yes, but we're not in our twenties, remember?" He lifted his eyebrows and shot a look at her that drove home his point.

She rolled her eyes and turned away from him. "Fine. Do you want lunch?"

"Have I ever turned down food?"

Something like a hiccup came from her, and a few moments later she started laughing. She'd been trying to hold it back, and a slow smile spread across Gage's face as the sound of her happiness filled the air.

Oh, yes, she was definitely different when she wasn't skittish. Wasn't scared. Wasn't scowling.

Now he just had to figure out how to stay on this good side of Sheryl until he figured out how to tell her she made his heart beat in a way it hadn't in a long time.

"We have to run over to my parents before we go tonight," she said.

"All right," he said, that heart of his kicking out extra beats. "What for?"

"My dad loves my meatloaf, and I made him an extra one last night."

"I thought you were taking that this morning." Gage dropped his backpack on her loveseat and sat beside it.

Sheryl remained silent, which drew Gage's attention. "You didn't go?"

"Ricky was here this morning. He tried to talk to me."

Instantly, Gage was on his feet and moving into the kitchen with her. "Sheryl, you're supposed to call me if he comes around when I'm not here."

She wouldn't look at him. "I know, but I took care of it."

"Did you? What makes you think that?"

Sheryl looked up at him, her blue-blue eyes firing like lasers. "I told him I'd call the police if I saw him hanging around again."

She'd told him that Ricky had asked her out several times, and she'd said no. When he'd started pestering a couple of waitresses at the on-site restaurant at the inn, she'd fired him. Oh, and he hadn't shown up for work three days in a row.

Her reasons for terminating him had seemed on the up-and-up, and Gage hadn't questioned her further.

"Honey, this guy doesn't care about the police," Gage said.

"Don't call me honey."

Gage fell back a step at the sharpness in her words. The anger in her face faded quickly, and she ducked her head. "Sorry, that came out harsher than I intended."

His heart shriveled, and he had no idea what to do

about that. So he said nothing and put more distance between them. What a fool he was. Just because he'd kissed her and it had been fantastic didn't mean they were a couple. She was paying him to babysit her, for crying out loud. He couldn't forget that.

Maybe he better start telling himself that to begin with.

"It's fine," he said, returning to the loveseat.

"I asked him what he was doing parked outside my house the other night. He said he was working on the water main at the Oscarson's."

"He's a liar," Gage said.

"How do you know?"

"I've already been next door, and they said they did have some trouble with their water line, but they'd never seen Ricky before."

Sheryl joined him in the living room, a plate with a ham and cheese sandwich on it. She handed it to him, and he looked up to meet her eyes. Something charged and electric passed between them, and if she didn't feel that, she had to be dead.

He took the plate as a blush stained her cheeks, and he knew she felt something. How much and what, he wasn't sure.

"When did you talk to them?"

"The day you hired me," he said. "I'm nothing if not thorough."

She nodded and folded her hands in her lap. "Thank

you, Gage. The last few afternoons have been much… better for me." She drew in a deep breath as he took the first bite of his sandwich.

A groan of satisfaction came up his throat at the salty ham and creamy cheese. After swallowing he said, "I'm going to hire you to be my private chef."

Sheryl trilled out a laugh. "It's a ham sandwich."

"It's good," he said, taking another bite. He didn't miss her smile or the look of pleasure in her eyes. Now, if he could just get her to look at him like that before he kissed her again….

Driving the thoughts from his mind, he said, "So you've told me a lot about your family. I haven't said much about mine."

"Oh, story time." She got up quickly. "Just a sec. Let me get the chips and sodas." She hurried back into the kitchen and started gathering things. A minute later, they both had sodas on the coffee table in front of them, along with a bag of chips, and Sheryl had a sandwich too.

"Okay, go," she said.

"It's all quite boring," he said. "I'm the oldest, and I have one younger brother."

"Shocking that you're the oldest," she said, and he paused to look at her to see if she was teasing him. Flirting with him.

And she totally was. That beautiful redness returned to her face, and she focused on the potato chips in front of her.

She reached up and took out the ponytail holder keeping that silky blonde hair on top of her head, and Gage's mouth went dry as it tumbled down to her shoulders.

With the prolonged silence, she looked at him, and Gage flinched. "We both went into the military, like our old man. My dad died overseas about, oh, let's see. I was fifteen. Michael was eleven."

"Twenty-four years ago," she said.

"Yeah." Gage's chest tightened. "That sounds right. We loved our dad, but he was a hard taskmaster. With him gone, Mom sort of fell apart, and I had to take over a lot of responsibilities around the house."

"Is that how you learned to bake?"

He chuckled and shook his head. "No, my grams had been teaching me for years. I still think it was a great disappointment to her when I chose the Marines over pastry school."

Sheryl smiled at him, and that moment felt very real and very comforting.

He cleared his throat and reached for his soda. The satisfying pop-and-hiss of opening the can filled the air between them, and he took a long drink. "It was Grams who taught me about the finer things in life," he said. "When to dress up, even if the occasion doesn't require it. She took us boys to symphonies and plays and weddings, even if she didn't know the people."

He laughed then, a keen sense of missing flowing

through him at the same time. "She died a while back too. Maybe ten years. I'm not great with dates."

"That's surprising," she said.

"Is it?"

"Yeah," she said. "You're so good at details. You'd think you'd know when the people you loved most departed." Her voice came out soft and gentle, and Gage sure did like the sound of it.

"Yeah, I guess," he said, because she was right.

"Do you miss your dad?"

"All the time," he said. "That's something that people lie to you about. They say time heals things, but it's not really true. Time just teaches you how resilient you are. How much you can handle, even when you think you can't."

Sheryl nodded as if she understood, but Gage didn't see how she could. She still had both of her parents.

He drew in a deep breath to cleanse his mind. "What are we doing this afternoon before the bonfire?" He'd gotten a teenager down the beach from him to come get Britta that day, so he didn't have the dog with him—and nothing to do except entertain his fantasies.

"I'm going to go shower," she said. "And start rooting through my closet for a sundress." She stilled and looked at him. "Do you think that's dressy enough for the bonfire?"

"Yeah, sure," he said. "I brought a simple pair of slacks and a button-up shirt." He smiled at her, hoping he wasn't pressuring her to do something she didn't want to do. "So we're napping, is that it?"

She giggled, and he once again thought she might be flirting with him. "You can nap if you want," she said.

"Thanks, butternut," he said, his eyes already drifting closed. She didn't respond, and Gage couldn't believe how comfortable he was here in Sheryl's house. With her. But he was, and he might have already drifted to sleep, because he imagined the touch of her fingertips along his shoulder as she walked past to go shower.

Ah, what a nice dream this was.

5

"He's not my boyfriend," Sheryl muttered to her mother for the third time. "I hired him to help me with a problem, and we're just going to the bonfire tonight. That's all."

"The bonfire," her mom said. "That's...romantic."

"Mom, stop." She turned from the fridge, where she'd taken far too long to find the bottle of ketchup. "You just heat this at four hundred degrees for about an hour," she said in a much louder voice.

Gage had sat at the table with her grandmother, who was currently educating him on the finer points of gin rummy. His face looked alert and bright, and Sheryl couldn't help how handsome she found him.

He's your bodyguard, she reminded herself, even if she had started to think about him more than normal. In fact, that afternoon, she'd had to shampoo her hair twice because she couldn't remember if she'd done it yet. Gage had consumed her brain power in the soft moments before she fell asleep too, and she woke with him as her first thought.

So maybe she had a crush on him. Didn't mean he was right for her. He said things in a way that made her feel stupid, and no woman wanted a boyfriend they had to pay to keep around.

Giving herself a mental shake as well as a physical one, she stepped over to Gage. "We should go so we're not late."

"Late for what?" he asked, barely glancing up.

Frustration filled Sheryl. The man really didn't get social cues at all. Sure, he might be able to see the exit points in a room, see the people trying to hide, conduct interviews with neighbors without her knowing. But he needed to learn how to read a room, because she was desperate to leave, and he had no clue.

"Dinner," she clipped out between her teeth. Her mother stood too close, her ears too open to every sound.

Gage looked up again, confusion in those beautiful eyes. In a snap of time, realization hit him. "Oh, right." He set down the cards he'd been holding and focused on her grandmother again. "We'll have to take this up another time, lovely." He beamed at her. "So great to meet you."

Her grandmother actually blushed as she reached up to pat her perfectly curled hair. "Oh, my."

Sheryl rolled her eyes, especially when she turned and found her mother grinning like the dang Cheshire cat.

"Come on," she said to Gage before she practically stomped across the living room to the front door. His voice sounded behind her, but it was too deep and too soft for her to make out the words.

She burst onto the porch, needing some fresh, cool air. She got air, but it was hot and filled with the scent of sand and surf and salt and something a bit decayed. A few moments later, Gage joined her, his hand slipping easily along her waist as he guided her down the steps.

"Sorry about that," he said. "Your grandmother is a real character. I was so engrossed in the game."

"You need to get out more," she said.

He chuckled, and she tried not to focus on the throaty quality of it. Or how heat was spreading out from the point of contact on her hip. Or how good he smelled, which didn't seem fair at all in that moment.

"So we're going to dinner?" he asked as he handed her a helmet. When she'd asked him where he'd gotten it, he'd said he'd bought it for her. Yesterday.

When he had time to do things like that, she wasn't sure. He worked until one, and he'd been at the inn, freshly showered and ready to do whatever she wanted by two. He'd been staying until ten or eleven too, and there was no way the motorcycle shop was open that late.

She fit it over her head, wishing she hadn't spent so much time on her hair that afternoon. Didn't matter. No matter what she did with her locks, they always ended up limp and stick-straight in a couple of hours. The helmet might actually help with the volume.

"I can't—" she started just as Gage's fingers covered hers and started to help with the strap that went under her chin. He didn't look at her, and he became a sexy, strong, *soft* man in that moment.

"What do you want for dinner?" he asked quietly as he finished with her helmet and turned to put on his.

"I don't know," she said, the words falling from her mouth without direct instruction from her brain. And she really didn't. In that moment, she didn't know much of anything.

"Let's go to Pie Squared," he said. "They're fast, and you haven't been there yet." He swung his leg over his motorcycle and gripped the handlebars.

"Okay." Sheryl hitched up her dress to climb on behind him, her heart pounding in her chest the same way it had when he'd told her they'd be taking the bike that night. She'd never been much of a motorcycle rider, though plenty of people used them around the island. They were one of the best ways to get around Carter's Cove, especially when the crowds swelled in the summer months.

But he'd taught her how and where to sit, how to lean with him, and how to hold onto him. She wrapped her arms around him and pressed her cheek to his back.

"Ready?" he asked, turning his head though he couldn't possibly see her.

He felt warm and solid and real in front of her, and Sheryl loved how grounded she felt on this motorcycle, with this man. She knew her mother and grandmother were probably watching, but she decided she didn't care.

"Ready."

He eased them away from the curb, keeping the engine rumbling nicely instead of filling the air with the sharp roar of it. He didn't turn left the way she expected him to, but went right instead, winding down the neighborhood streets to the coastal highway.

A sense of wonder and freedom filled Sheryl, and she couldn't keep the smile off her face. Riding in the open air like this made her feel alive in a way she hadn't felt in a long time, and she loosened her grip on his body and straightened so she could feel the sea breeze against her face.

Laughter tumbled from her chest, and she put her hands on his waist to steady herself. His laughter joined hers, but she could barely hear it. Didn't matter. She could feel it in his body, and when he accelerated, she whooped with joy.

By the time they arrived at the bonfire, Sheryl's adrenaline rush had faded. They'd enjoyed dinner at Pie Squared, and he hadn't been lying. The pizza was fantastic, and she'd eaten way too much.

Her pulse spiked again as Gage took her helmet and stowed it in his saddlebag before taking her hand in his.

"Is this okay?" he asked, and Sheryl had no idea what to say. She looked around as if she were important enough to have paparazzi behind her, snapping pictures of every person she even looked at.

No one cared that she was holding hands with the gorgeous, dangerous, mysterious Gage Sanders.

"It's fine," she said.

"Oh-ho," he chuckled. "Must not be okay then." He started to pull his fingers out of hers, but she held onto them tightly.

"It is."

"I've had other girlfriends," he said bluntly. "And when they said something was fine, it definitely wasn't."

"How many other girlfriends?" she asked, sliding her fingers between his and holding on.

He grinned at her. "Several. No one since I moved here permanently, though. Well, there was this one woman." He shrugged. "But she didn't live here."

"Name?"

"Dana O'Shiel."

"Yeah, I don't know her."

He tugged her closer to him as they approached a couple coming their way. "I said she didn't live here."

"Plus, it's not like I know everyone on the island. Pretty much only if someone grew up here and stayed, the way I have." She pointed down the boardwalk. "For example, the band playing tonight is all locals. Some a couple of years older than me or younger than me. I only knew the banjo player."

"Mm," he said, reaching for a tumbler of water as a waiter paused. "You want something to drink?"

"Just club soda," she said, and the waiter pointed to the wet bar that had been set up on the sand. Sheryl glanced around and saw that almost everyone there had dressed up a little bit, and she was so glad she'd found this splashy sundress in the back of her closet.

It left her shoulders a little barer than she normally liked them, but as the sun drifted down, she wasn't afraid of getting burnt.

Gage led them over to the bar, where he ordered club soda for both of them, his with lime and lemon and orange. His glass looked colorful and vibrant, and Sheryl thought it fit him really well.

She never would've imagined the Gage she'd met on her front porch at an event like this, but he fit in seam-lessly with that button up shirt undone at the throat and his sandaled feet. They strolled along the boardwalk closer to the band, and she pointed with her glass. "That's Mat Lindstrom right there, with the banjo." She grinned at the man she'd been friends with for many years, searching the crowd for his wife.

Sheryl was friends with Lindsey too, and while they had just had their first baby, they still invited Sheryl to dinner sometimes. All of her married friends did, and she cut a look out of the corner of her eye at Gage. Maybe she could start bringing him to lunches and dinners and picnics on the beach. Maybe she could be part of a couple again.

Her heart seized, and Gage looked at her as if he could tell her vital organ had skipped a few beats. "What's wrong?" He didn't search the surroundings but kept his gaze right on hers.

"Nothing," she said. "I was just thinking about my last boyfriend."

"Oh, that's not what I want to hear." He gave her a smile. "I mean, we're here together. This band is great. The moon is coming up. No man wants to hear the beautiful woman he's with is thinking about another guy." He lifted his fruity club soda to his lips, those dark eyes devouring her.

Beautiful woman he's with.

"So before the disaster that has become Ricky—"

"Wait," Gage said. "Your last boyfriend was the stalker?"

"No." She shook her head. "No, I never went out with him. He just asked me a bunch of times."

Gage nodded and said, "Continue," as if this were an interrogation.

Annoyance squirreled through her. "I don't want to tell it now."

"Oh, come on," he said, practically rolling his whole head. "What did I do?"

"You just were like, 'continue,' like all of your demands would be satisfied before I said another word."

Gage's eyes sparkled like dark diamonds, and dang if Sheryl didn't want to lean closer and see what he found so funny. "Well," he drawled in that Savannah-accent. "Won't all my demands be satisfied tonight?" He leaned closer, sending Sheryl's pulse into a complete tizzy.

"No." She pushed against his chest, laughing in the next moment. "I don't even know what your demands are, so they definitely won't all be satisfied."

"Mm," he said again, touching his nose to her cheek for a moment before straightening and backing up. "You can keep telling the story whenever you're ready."

"Thank you, your highness."

He scoffed, but not an ounce of discomfort or unease sat on his face.

Sheryl wasn't sure how to pick up the story again. "Anyway," she said. "Before Ricky, I dated this guy named Chuck Millstone. I thought things were going well, but so did his other girlfriend."

"Ouch," Gage said without missing a beat. "And Chuck is a stupid name."

Surprise shot through her, and she burst out laughing. "It is, isn't it? I mean, no offense to the nice Chuck's out there."

The one she'd dated had not been nice. In fact, he'd accused her of trying to change him, and that was why he'd had to go find another girlfriend who "loved him just how he was."

Gage grinned at her, and time seemed to freeze. The moonlight was romantic. The bluegrass band had started a slow song.

"Do you want to dance?" Gage asked, and there was nothing more exciting to Sheryl in that moment than the idea of dancing with the ex-Marine, bodyguard-slash-boyfriend, sexy man in front of her.

"Sure," she said at the same time someone else said, "Sheryl?"

She startled, immediately stepping away from Gage who fell a half-step behind her. Her oldest sister stood there, a delicious-looking man on her arm too. "Olympia." Her eyes flickered to the tall, sandy-haired man at her sister's side.

"This is Chet," she said, looking up at him.

"Gage," she said, and Olympia shook the man's hand.

"Nice to meet you," Olympia said, her eyes grinning as if they knew what Sheryl had been thinking about dancing with Gage. "What are you guys doing here?"

"It's the bonfire," Sheryl said. "I wanted to get out of the house tonight." Her sister wasn't dim, and Sheryl stared at her, hoping to communicate that she should wrap up this conversation so Sheryl could get her dance before the song ended.

Olympia simply smiled at her sister. "It's great, isn't it?" She hadn't been out with anyone in years, and if she was really dating Chet, Sheryl was happy for her. Olympia's last boyfriend had cheated on her too, but not only that, he'd been married while they were dating.

Married.

She looked at Chet again, and it sure seemed like there were plenty of sparks there.

"I really like the band," Sheryl said. "Did you know the banjo player is Mat Lindstrom, from high school?"

"Really?" Olympia asked. "I didn't recognize him."

Chet leaned closer to her, and she turned her head so he could whisper in her ear. He said something, she nodded, and he walked away. Olympia watched him, interest evident in her eyes, and Sheryl grinned at her sister.

"What's with you two?" Sheryl asked, leaning closer. "You've never said you're seeing someone new."

"I'm still trying to figure out what we are." Olympia glanced at Gage, leaning in and whispering too, though Gage seemed totally engrossed in the band and the crowd around them. A front, Sheryl knew. The man heard and saw everything. Literally everything. "I'm sure you know what I mean."

Sheryl just blinked. "I have no idea what you mean." And yet, she found herself inching back into Gage, who put his arm around her, his hand resting easily on her hip.

Olympia looked like a cat who'd just gotten his first canary. "Hmm."

The song was almost over, and Sheryl was going to

miss it. "See you later, O." She turned into Gage and said, "Let's dance."

He obliged, and though they only got thirty seconds, they were thirty of the best seconds of Sheryl's life, dancing in the arms of her...bodyguard.

6

age adored the feel of this woman in his arms. "I think you're going to want to kiss me again," he whispered, but Sheryl just stared at him.

"Why would I want to do that?" she asked, though everything about tonight said she wanted to do that. From the sexy dress she wore, to the way she'd tried to get him away from her mother and grandmother, to the way she'd practically cemented herself to him on that motorcycle.

"Because Ricky's here, and he's not alone."

She tensed in his arms, scanning the crowd now. "Where? I haven't seen him."

"I saw him the moment we arrived," Gage said. And he had. He'd moved them to the wet bar and then into the crowd, hoping Ricky would get the hint and leave. He certainly wasn't going to make a move in public. Gage knew that. The other man was too much of a coward for that.

"He's over there with a couple of other guys. They look like they might be brothers." He nodded toward the side of the party they hadn't visited yet, and Sheryl had to hold onto his shoulders as she twisted to look behind her.

She sucked in a breath as she faced him again, her eyes filled with worry now. "Don't look like that, honeybee," he said. "He can't touch you while you're with me."

She swallowed and nodded, saying, "But I'm not always with you."

Gage looked down at her, his feelings for her new, sure. But very real. And swelling with every minute they spent together. He couldn't explain it. On paper, they were not a match. Heck, sometimes in person they were not a match. He barked. She quipped.

The song had ended, but she still stood in his arms, a desperate look on her face. "Let's get out of here," he said, not quite what he'd been hoping to accomplish by telling her about Ricky and his bros. Cronies. Whoever they were.

He cast the other man a long look as he put his arm around Sheryl and guided her off the sand and back to the boardwalk. They didn't speak as they walked away, and because he owned a motorcycle, they didn't have to wait for a pedicab or to get their car from the valet.

"Where do you want to go?" he asked. "Home?"

"Maybe we could tour your place," she said, buckling her helmet on. She was adorable in the way her fingers couldn't see to latch things right, and he once again helped her, feeling the weight of those eyes on his face as he did.

He cast her a quick smile, because he'd gotten the hint that she did not want to kiss him again. Why was it the only thing he could think about?

"My place?" Fear rushed through him. "Oh, sweetheart, I don't know about that."

"Why not?"

He met her eye then. "I live on the beach too, but let's just say it's not the five-star cottage you have."

A determined glint entered her eyes. "I want to see it."

He sighed, the sound lengthening as he pressed the air out of his lungs. "Fine. Let's go see it." He swung his leg over the bike and waited for her to hike up her skirt and climb on behind him. He hadn't ridden with a woman on the back of his motorcycle for far too long, and he sure did like the addition of Sheryl to his life.

It was a quick ride away from the bonfire to his shack on the beach, and thankfully, he'd learned to leave a light on when he left in the afternoons. He'd been staying at Sheryl's late, and it was dark out on this lane.

"This is cute," she said as she got off the motorcycle. From inside the house, Britta barked, and Gage left their helmets on the handlebars instead of stowing them away.

He had neighbors out here, sure, but no one would bother the bike.

"Cute?" he asked, adding a growl to the word though her assessment of his house didn't really bother him.

"I mean, it's dark," Sheryl said. "But it looks cute."

"It's cute enough, I guess." He went up the few steps to the front door and opened it to receive Britta, who sniffed him like he'd cheated on her by going to the bonfire and dancing with Sheryl. "Back up, Britt," he said. "Go on."

The beach house wasn't anything impressive, but it had all the essential rooms. Living room big enough to hold a couch and a recliner. TV. Curtains on the windows. A kitchen, bathroom, and two bedrooms down the hall. Oh, and the beach out the back door. He loved that the most.

"See?" He glanced around. "Smaller than yours. Dirtier. And nothing good to eat in the fridge." He chuckled, surprised at how nervous he was to have her there.

Sheryl looked around—but not up at the ceiling—and said, "It's nice, Gage."

"I do have ice cream."

"Sold." She grinned at him, and he moved over to the freezer to get out the sweet treat.

"We can sit on the back porch and hear the waves."

"Oh, so you're much closer to the ocean than I am."

"Yep." He grabbed two spoons from the utensil drawer and didn't bother with bowls. They settled on the steps, the full moon shining on the water and the sand, casting a silver glow over the world.

"It's beautiful out here," she said, her voice full of awe.

Gage dug into the mint chocolate chip and said, "Sure is," before putting the bite into his mouth. But he wasn't even looking at the moon. Just Sheryl. He swallowed, his taste buds in overdrive now with the ice cream still coating his mouth. "You know, you're going to have to stop running away every time you see Ricky."

She flinched and looked at him with accusation in her eyes. "I did not run away. You're the one who said we should go."

"You were uncomfortable."

"How do you know that?"

"Sheryl, I can see everything you're thinking and feeling, right there in your eyes." And she was angry now, though he'd spoken as quietly and gently as he could.

She looked away, and Gage kicked himself mentally for bringing it up. "Maybe we should file a restraining order," he said. "Just as an added layer of protection."

"I'm not stupid," she said.

Gage felt her retreat fully from him, and he sighed. "I didn't say you were stupid."

"You implied it."

"How did I possibly do that?"

"You said I should file a restraining order, as if I'd never thought of that."

"Have you thought of it?"

"Yes."

"And?"

"*And* I researched it," she said, the volume of her voice lifting into the starry sky. "And he hasn't done anything that would warrant a restraining order. No judge would give me one."

Gage simply nodded, wondering how this conversation had gone sideways so fast. She stabbed at the ice cream, and Gage let her. He didn't want another bite anyway. He let the waves push and pull his thoughts, because speaking to Sheryl always seemed to get him in trouble.

"Grams used to say that on nights like these, you could catch fairies. They liked to come out and dance under the light of the full moon." Where the words had come from, Gage wasn't sure.

Several long seconds went by, and finally Sheryl asked, "Did you ever catch one?"

Their eyes met, and the awkwardness broke between them. He chuckled and ducked his head, and she giggled.

"Not even close," Gage whispered, hoping he hadn't ruined his chances with the only woman who'd caught his eye in the past couple of years.

THE NEXT DAY, GAGE WATCHED THE SAME MAN RIDE THE ferry back and forth twice before he approached the guy. "Where are you going?" he asked him, folding his arms.

The man glanced up, but his sunglasses obscured his eyes. Gage stared down at him. "You've been on the ferry a lot today."

"Is that a problem?" he asked.

"It is if there's something unsafe going on."

"Sit down," the guy said, glancing around.

Gage hesitated for a moment, and he followed the other man's gaze. A woman sat down on the end of the bench. Gage sat down. "Stalking?"

"No," the man said quickly. "I just know she rides the ferry over to the mainland to work, and I wanted to see if I could talk to her today."

"And she missed the previous ferry."

"I guess," he said.

"Have you ever talked to her?" Gage asked.

The man shook his head, and though the sun shone brightly overhead, Gage thought he'd started to blush. "She lives down the road from me. I'm just...look, I'm not doing anything wrong."

Considering Gage had been hired to take Sheryl home so the man following her couldn't do anything funny, he wasn't sure he agreed. "You talk to her today," he said. "And stop following her around."

"I don't follow her around," he said. "I work on the mainland too, and I've just noticed her on the ferry."

"All right," Gage said in a tone that clearly said he didn't believe the guy. He stood up and went back around the ferry, taking his time. The ferry ride took thirty minutes, and they'd been on the water for ten minutes.

He rounded the back of the ferry, where the dark-haired woman still sat, her e-reader in her hand, all of her attention on it. The man sat down the bench several paces, his focus on his own device.

"Ma'am," he said. "There's a leak back here, and I've been asked to move everyone up a little bit."

She glanced up at him, and he pointed down the bench. "Just down there would be fine. I'm going to be setting some stuff up here." It almost sounded true.

"Sure," she said. "Thanks for letting me know." She gathered her purse and bag and got up, stepping down the bench a little bit. The man who'd ridden the ferry just to talk to her glanced up as she sat so much closer to him.

Gage saw the panic on his face, and then it melted into a smile as he reached over and moved his briefcase. He looked up and Gage touched his forehead in a quick salute before turning to go into the engine room to actually get a bucket. He didn't need that woman knowing he'd helped out the guy semi-following her.

The rest of his shift was fairly uneventful, and he even survived Walker's few questions about how the bonfire had gone. At one point, Gage had thought the night was ruined. But after his mention of fairies, things had improved, and Sheryl had given him a tight squeeze before she'd slid off his motorcycle and disappeared through the front door of her house.

And Ricky hadn't been parked out front, so Gage was counting the night as a win.

Now he just needed to figure out how to move out of bodyguard territory and into the boyfriend zone.

7

*S*heryl's fingers ached after holding the rope so tight while Javier drove stakes into the ground so they could straighten this row of trees. The winds coming off the water could murder, and these four-year-old trees needed some support to help them grow straight and tall. That was, if Mother Nature didn't send a hurricane to wipe them all out.

"Almost got it," he said, taking the rope from her and pulling it even further. How he did that, she wasn't sure. She thought she was strong—and she knew she was. It took muscles to lug around bags of gravel and bark, bend and squat and dig and prune.

She loved every minute of it—except when her fingers hurt like this. Her mother had arthritis, and Sheryl suspected she probably did too. With how much she used her hands during the day, it wouldn't be surprising.

"Okay," she said, exhaling as she looked down the sidewalk. "Only seventy more."

Javier laughed, and Sheryl smiled. There weren't seventy more trees to do. It just felt like it. "How's Melinda?" she asked as they moved down to the next tree.

"She's doing okay," Javier said. He'd been with The Heartwood Inn grounds crew for as long as Sheryl could remember. She'd thrown a wedding shower and then a baby shower for his wife, and their first baby was due any day now. "She's taken to walking morning and night, trying to induce labor."

"Does that really work?" Sheryl asked.

"Obviously not." Javier flashed her a grin. "I'm still okay to have time off when the baby does come, right?"

"Of course," Sheryl said. She had an entire temporary crew lined up to prepare the beach for the upcoming surfing championship. She could get whoever she needed to stay on while Javier was gone. "You're missing the best part of the year, though."

"You're such a liar." He ran his hands up the tree trunk, and Sheryl felt his love for the tree. She felt the same way, as she'd always been comfortable at home caring for plants, flowers, trees, and shrubs. "Raking the beach is the *worst* time of the year."

"Oh, come on," she said. "You're telling me you're going to miss the banana split party we have when it's finally done?" She handed out bonuses during that party too. She knew raking and landscaping sand that would just get destroyed once all the spectators showed up was a torturous job.

She paid well, and she never had a problem getting extra men on the crew. She always gave out a little extra cash upon completion to everyone, and some got more than a little. They had prizes and contests, Sheryl worked as hard as her crew did.

"Can I come to the banana split party and just skip the raking?"

"I think I might have a mutiny on my hands if you did that." Sheryl pulled the rope again, and Javier sized up where to put the stake.

"Well, let's hope the baby comes after the surfing competition then," he said. "I do like the banana split party."

"I knew it."

"And you should come to dinner soon," he said. "Melinda is in full nesting mode, and she cooks all day long."

"Maybe she's trying to entice your son out with the scent of good Mexican food."

Javier laughed, the sound filling this quiet patch of the resort. "Maybe. That doesn't seem to be working either, but I'm eating well."

"What's she making tonight?" Sheryl wondered if she could take Gage. How would she introduce him? He'd talked about kissing again last night, but they hadn't done that. After they'd left the bonfire, things between them had turned strained, though he'd managed to lighten the evening with talk of fairies, of all things.

He was an enigma to her. Sometimes he could be the kindest, most charming man she'd ever met. And sometimes he was simply annoying. Rough around the edges. Tactless. He was handsome, though, and strong, and sexy, and she liked that he had a past she didn't know about yet.

It was that past that hid the true man underneath that held her interest and kept her from writing him off completely, though he did rub her the wrong way at least fifty percent of the time.

"Sopapillas," Javier said.

"Isn't that a dessert?"

"I didn't hear the main dish," he said, taking the rope from her. She shook out her hands as he leaned his weight into the rope and secured it to the stake. "Once she said sopapillas, I stopped listening."

"You're terrible," she said with a laugh.

He laughed too, noticing how she rotated her wrists. "You okay?"

"Fine." She smiled at him. "And I think I will come tonight, if I can bring a...friend."

Javier's whole face lit up. "A friend? What kind of friend?"

"Oh, don't get excited," Sheryl said, instantly regretting that she'd said anything. "He's actually my bodyguard. Ricky's been following me around the island."

A storm crossed her friend's face. "Ricky Van Nuy?

What a loser." He took off his work gloves and pulled out his phone. "Want me to talk to him?"

"No," she said. "I've already taken care of it." When he looked doubtful, she said, "Really. So use that thing to text Melinda and say I'll be there with my bodyguard, Gage."

"Gage Sanders?"

"You know him?"

"Sure," Javier said, focusing on his phone. "My dad's used him for security a couple of times at the water park." His family owned the park here on the island, and they hosted four huge concerts every year that Sheryl assumed they probably needed extra security for. "Nice guy."

"Is he?" Sheryl cocked her head and watched as Javier finished his text.

"You don't think so?" He looked at her, searching for something Sheryl was sure he'd find. Gage had said she wore everything on her face.

She looked away quickly. "I mean, he's got quite the bark."

"Bark is good for a security guard," he said. "And a bodyguard."

"True," she said, turning away to get another length of rope. This conversation needed to end, right now. Because Javier was absolutely right. Gage's loud bark was extremely good for a bodyguard—just not for a boyfriend.

Sheryl finished with the trees. Finished her paperwork. Finished her work for the day completely. She needed to stop by Olympia's office to give her an update—and find out what was going on with her and the delicious drink of water she'd been with last night.

So she washed up and made sure she didn't have a piece of errant bark in her hair before going upstairs to her sister's office. She didn't bother to knock as she opened the door, and she found her sister sitting at her desk, a bowl of salad in front of her. Typical Olympia. Eating lunch at almost two o'clock in the afternoon.

"Oh, hey," she said, mixing in her pine nuts, goat cheese, and cherry tomatoes. "What's up?"

"I wanted to talk to you for a minute." Sheryl sighed as she sat in the chair across from Olympia. Her body hurt, and she might have to concede and take some pain medication.

"How was the bonfire last night?" Olympia asked, taking a bite of her salad.

Sheryl didn't want to talk about the bonfire. Not really. "It was fun." Her voice sounded false, even to her.

Olympia swallowed, her expression turning stern and older-sisterly. "I saw you holding Gage's hand."

"Yeah, well." Sheryl shrugged, heat crawling up her neck. Things had gone well at the bonfire. It was after that they'd turned south. "He thinks it'll keep Ricky further away, but it doesn't seem to be working."

"No? I think it's working with something, Sher." She lifted her eyebrows, a wicked grin forming on her face.

Sheryl shook her head. "He's my bodyguard, not my boyfriend." She wondered how many times she'd have to make that defense.

"Yeah, maybe you should practice saying that with more conviction," Olympia teased. "And maybe tell him, so he stops holding your hand in public." She took another bite of her salad as Sheryl started laughing. She really hadn't said the words with much conviction.

"He's kind of...overbearing," she said, thinking maybe this could be a conversation about how to be in a relationship instead of an update on her stalker.

Olympia set her salad aside, the conversation turning real. "But you still like him." She wasn't asking, and Sheryl appreciated that her sister would take time from her crazy schedule to talk to her about a personal matter. Olympia always had, though.

"Maybe," Sheryl said, confused about how she felt about Gage. Why couldn't he just be Prince Charming and sweep her off her feet? "I don't know."

"Where'd you find him?"

"He came highly recommended," Sheryl said. "He's worked private security for events on the island for a couple years. I called him, and he was available in the evenings."

"I bet he was." Olympia grinned in a wicked way. "Did you send him your picture before he accepted the job?"

Sheryl rolled her eyes, now ready to leave the office. Gage would be here any minute anyway. "No, I did not."

"Did you get his picture? Because I bet you think he's *gorgeous.*"

Sheryl did think he was gorgeous, but she didn't want to admit it. So she shrugged one shoulder and said, "Maybe."

"Oh, but he's your bodyguard," Olympia teased. "And he's kind of annoying."

"He's been taking me home for a couple of nights," Sheryl said. "I barely know him."

"Does he stay over?"

"No," Sheryl said. "Ricky's sort of backed off."

"Tell me about this Ricky. We employed him?"

"For a few weeks," Sheryl said, somewhat relieved to be back on topic. She felt whiplashed all over the place. First, she wanted to talk about Gage. Then she didn't. "His name is Ricky—Rick—Richard Van Nuy. He said he was working on a water main for the Oscarson's. That was why he was parked outside my cottage."

Olympia frowned and picked a nut off her salad. "But they live quite a bit down the road."

"I know. He said the water line was right on the edge of our property."

"And is it?"

"I don't know. I didn't see it, and Gage said Ricky didn't know what he was doing." Sheryl sat back in her chair.

"Anyway, I just came to update you on that. And to ask you about Chet. Did you figure out what you are?"

Olympia went mute, clearly inside her own mind. "Not really," she said, but Sheryl started laughing before she'd even finished speaking.

"I can see it in your face, sis," she said. "You kissed him."

Olympia looked like she'd swallowed the most delicious treat in the world. "Maybe."

"Good for you. It's been way too long since you've been out with someone." Sheryl knew what Olympia had been through. She'd had her own version of a man cheating on her, though it wasn't nearly to the same degree as Olympia. Still, she knew that wounds like that took a very long time to heal, and the simplest of things could reopen them.

"I know," she said. "We're...he's going to work for the inn next week during the surfing competition. I'm getting to know him. That's what we are."

"And you get to kiss him good-night," Sheryl said. "Sounds like a sweet set-up." And she suddenly wanted that set-up too. A bodyguard-slash-boyfriend who picked her up from work *and* kissed her goodnight.

"Yeah." Olympia pulled her lunch back in front of her and glanced at her laptop, code for *I need to get back to work.*

"Okay, well, I'm going to go home," Sheryl said. "Gage

should be here any minute. He works the ferry in the morning."

"Oh, wow. Those start running at six."

"Yeah, he's ex-military. Says he doesn't need as much sleep as normal humans." Sheryl laughed, because Gage didn't seem to do anything the same as normal humans.

Olympia smiled, got up, and gave her a hug. "If you like him, honey, he could be your bodyguard *and* your boyfriend."

"Jury's still out," she said, her phone chiming. As she checked it, everything happy inside her died, replaced with only annoyance. "See? Look at this text. What am I supposed to get from that?"

She gave the phone to Olympia so she could see what Gage had said. *Are you ready? I've been here for five minutes and don't see you. Want to go to lunch?*

"Is he annoyed with me?" she asked. "Because I'm not standing on the curb the moment he pulls up? Like, I don't need that in my life."

She didn't want to be bossed around. She ran a grounds crew of sixty-four people. Maybe she didn't get done with work right at two o'clock, right on the dot.

"I think he's asking you to lunch?" Olympia handed the phone back. "Maybe he's just saying he's here, and he's been watching for you, and he wants to take you to lunch."

"Maybe." Sheryl headed for the door, frustrated. "I'll text you later." She opened the door to find the cause of her irritation standing in the hall. "Oh. Gage. I'm *coming*." Jeez. He'd come looking for her? What next? He'd go into the bathroom with her?

She stepped past him, not willing to snipe at him in front of Olympia, but there was a storm brewing in her chest, and he better watch out.

8

Gage waved to Olympia and turned to follow Sheryl down the hall. "I just hadn't heard from you."

"I was talking to my sister," Sheryl said. "I literally just got your text. Yes, I'm hungry. We can go to lunch."

Gage had a hard time keeping up with her, that blonde ponytail swaying violently as she marched away from him. So she was angry. Well, so was he. He jogged the last few steps to the door that led back down to the lower level of the inn, where her office was.

"Ricky is down there." He put his palm on the door so she couldn't pull it open. Her eyes finally looked up and into his, but she didn't look like the scared rabbit she'd been last night.

"Well, let's go see what he wants," she said.

Surprise arched his eyebrows. "Is that what you want to do?"

"You're the one who said I can't run away from him every time he shows his face."

"That's not exactly what I said."

"Move, Gage."

"Why are you so upset?"

She shook her phone at him. "You made it sound like waiting five minutes for me was a horrible crime against humanity." Her fury stormed across her face, but she was still drop-dead gorgeous. Maybe more so because of it.

Gage wanted to quip right back at her, but he drew in a slow breath first. "I thought you might have locked yourself in your office, Sheryl," he said, slowly and without any emotion whatsoever. "So I was a little worried. That's all."

The wind that had gotten her all bunched up deflated, and her shoulders slumped. "Is he really down there?"

"He really is." Gage removed his hand from the door. "And if you want to go talk to him, I'll go with you. But then I really do want to go to lunch. All the food trucks are going to South Port today."

Gage loved a good food truck. And he loved the vibe at South Port, where murals lined the storm surge walls with messages of hope and love for those who'd lost their lives in previous hurricanes and gales.

Sheryl frowned. "South Port?"

"Do you not grace the southern part of the island with your presence?" As soon as the words left his mouth, Gage knew he'd made a huge mistake. "Sorry," he said. "That was rude. Let's go talk to Ricky."

"And to think I was going to invite you to go to dinner with some friends of mine tonight." Sheryl yanked open the door, practically hitting him in the face.

He opened his mouth to retort, but nothing came out. "Wait. What?" But she was gone already, off to face Ricky alone, absolute anger in her footsteps flying down the steps. He hurried after her, though in that moment, he had no doubt that Sheryl Heartwood could take care of herself.

She was only a few paces ahead of him when he came out of the stairwell, and Ricky had stood from the chair he'd been waiting on.

"What are you doing here?" she demanded, her fingers curled into fists. "You're not allowed on the property, and I know you were following me on your bike the other day."

He was? Why hadn't Gage heard about that?

She came to a stop, and he went to her side, watching Ricky for any signs of sudden movement.

"I just wanted to talk to you," Ricky said, his eyes pleading when he looked at Sheryl. They turned hard when they moved to Gage. "Alone. Without your muscle."

"I'm not her muscle," Gage said. "She can take care of herself." He reached over and slid his hand around hers, working to uncurl those fingers. "She's my girlfriend. There's a difference."

Sheryl looked at him, searching for something. But he wasn't going to give her the answer right then. He'd dealt with men like Ricky before, and the best thing to do was stick to one idea. Never let the other person see how he felt.

"She told you no, man. More than once."

Ricky frowned, his eyes sparking with danger. He looked back at Sheryl. "I can't believe this meathead is your type."

Gage drew in a breath through his nose. He wasn't a meathead just because he'd served in the military instead of going to college. He didn't even frequent the gym that much, because six a.m. came early enough as it was.

"More so than you," she said, finally slipping her fingers through his. She squeezed, and Gage thought it might be more about her anger than her need for him. "Ricky, just go. Leave me alone. If you keep doing things like this, the police said I can have you brought in for questioning, and then I can get a restraining order."

She spoke in a less-than-angry voice, and Gage knew she didn't want all the hassle. Ricky stared at her for another few seconds, the tension drawing taut between them. "All right," he finally said. "You can call off the dog then." He threw Gage a dark look and turned to go.

Sheryl waited until the metal door closed behind Ricky, and then she wrenched her hand out of his. "Dog? What have you been doing?"

"Nothing," Gage said.

"He said I needed to call you off. Have you been bothering him?"

"No," Gage said. "I may have sent a patrol car by his place this morning. It was nothing."

Sheryl glared at him. "I can't believe you."

"Me?" he asked. "I didn't do anything wrong."

She went into her office and came back out with her purse. "I'd like to go home now."

"No lunch?"

"I don't feel like eating," she said.

"Who was dinner with tonight?" He moved in front of the door so she couldn't storm away from him again.

"Someone who works here with me," she said, refusing to look at him. The way she stared over his shoulder was unnerving and annoying. "His wife is about to have a baby, and she's an excellent cook."

Gage wanted to fix whatever had snapped between them. Last night, he'd said some stupid thing about fairies. Today, he had nothing. So he said, "Sheryl, I'm sorry. Okay?" He stepped forward and put his hand under her chin, guiding her gaze to his. "I'm sorry. I thought you wanted help with Ricky. I thought you might be in your office while he kept you there by being in that chair."

"And South Port?"

"I didn't think," Gage said.

"Because I go to South Port," she said, lifting that chin so his fingers didn't touch her skin anymore.

"I believe you." Though, he didn't really. South Port

was in a seedier part of the island, and not many tourists went down there either. The only thing to see was the murals and the beach, but there were many more miles of better beach along the southeast, eastern, and northern parts of the island.

"It's okay," he said. "I'll take you home, and you can decide about dinner. I'd like to go meet your friends." She hadn't said much about them, spending most of her time talking about her family. He turned and opened the door, stepping back to hold it open for her.

She kept her eyes on his as she passed, finally looking forward when she stepped outside. She got behind the wheel of her car while he mounted up on the bike. He didn't know what to think. Had he blown his shot of ever being more than "her muscle" or "her dog" because he'd said something rude about South Port?

Sheryl seemed to be able to forgive easily, and she felt things deeply. Maybe she just needed some time to get over what he'd said. *And you need to think before you speak,* he told himself as he followed her out of the parking lot and up the street toward her cottage.

The ten minute drive to her house passed quickly, with the sun beating down on the island and the wind barely a visitor that day. He got off his motorcycle and went with her up to the door. "I'm sorry again," he said. "Really. I'll have my phone with me, so text me if you want me to come back and go to dinner with you."

"I don't need to text you," she said, turning into him.

Only a couple of feet separated them, but it felt like miles to Gage. He couldn't look anywhere but into her eyes, and she couldn't seem to look away from him either.

Hesitantly, she reached up and cradled his face in the palm of her hand. "Javier said we can come at six."

Joy burst through Gage, causing a smile to form on his mouth. "Great," he said. "Do you want me to stay now? Or I can come back. I don't think Ricky will bother you anymore."

"Really? You believed him?"

"I honestly have no idea what to believe," Gage said. And thinking was so very hard with her hand still holding his face.

"Go get something for lunch at the food trucks," she said. "And then come back. But be warned. Melinda Garcia makes a mean sopapilla, and the spread of food there tonight will be epic."

"So don't eat too much now," he said, translating for her.

"Right." With that, Sheryl tipped up onto her toes, swept her lips across his other cheek, and darted into her house.

Gage stood on the porch, staring at whatever was in front of him. What in the world had just happened?

"She's hot and cold," he muttered to himself as he turned to look at the closed door, and then spun to walk down the steps to his bike. Truth was, he ran hot and cold too. A sentence could trigger him, and then he'd be angry. Sheryl seemed to be made of the same stuff, while he'd thought her to be his opposite before.

Thinking about it all just made him more confused, and he pushed every thought away as he put on his helmet. He just needed to ride. Let the wind and the birds at South Port tell him what to do.

So he set his bike north to go around the island the long way, and he just enjoyed the ride.

SOUTH PORT BUZZED WITH ENERGY, AND GAGE GOT A footlong with extra spicy brown mustard—his favorite lunch. He found a bench in the shade and sat down to enjoy the surf coming in. The wind. The birds. The people. The scent of something fried. He liked it all. He thought he might like it more with Sheryl beside him, but he wouldn't be asking her to come to the food truck rally at South Port again.

His phone rang, and he glanced at the number. "Michael." He hadn't heard from his brother in a couple of weeks, so he swiped on the call and set aside his hot dog. "Hey, bro."

"Gage." Michael laughed. "It's good to hear your voice."

"Yeah? Where you at?"

"Oh, I'm still home," he said. "Got a job with the cable

company for now. Marie and Maggie want you to come visit."

"Right." Gage scoffed. "Your wife and daughter want me to come?" He couldn't go, not without asking for a lot of time off. He could get to Peach Tree in a day, but then it was a day back, and if he stayed for only a day, that was three days of work. Almost a week.

Fine, not a week, but Gage hated going home.

Michael chuckled. "I'm actually thinking we need a vacation on the beach, and you live on Carter's Cove."

"Sure, come on over," he said. "The island is full of people right now, but it's a great place to spend a day on the beach." Or a week, as most families did.

"Okay," Michael said. "It's just me who needs a vacation on the beach."

Gage sat up straighter and glanced around like there might be someone eavesdropping on him. "Mike? What's going on? Give it to me straight."

"Marie asked me to leave for a little while," he said. "And I need somewhere to stay."

"Leave?"

"Move out," he clarified.

Gage blinked, unsure of what to say to his little brother. "I'm sorry. Yeah, uh, yeah. You can come stay with me. Tell me all about it."

"Okay." Michael sighed. "Wow, making this call sucked as hard as I thought it would." He laughed, but there was no joy in the sound. "Can I come tomorrow?"

"Sure," Gage said. "Of course."

"You still working the ferry in the morning?"

"Yes," Gage said. "But you stop by any time you want. Britta will be there, and I'll be home just after one." They continued making plans, and Gage hung up. His hot dog had long gone cold, and he didn't have an appetite for it anyway.

His brother was separating from his wife. "So strange," he muttered to the sea in front of him. Michael and Marie had always been rock-solid. Maggie, Gage's niece, was seven years old, and she adored her father. Gage had never seen a family so strong.

If they couldn't make things work, how could Gage ever expect to have a meaningful, lasting relationship?

Heck, he couldn't even send the right text to the woman he wanted.

9

*S*heryl changed out of her dirty clothes and showered before she collapsed into bed. Her thoughts revolved around Gage, and several minutes passed before she was able to drift off to sleep.

Problem was, the man starred in her dreams too, and he was always the thoughtful, vulnerable, apologetic man she'd seen a few times now. When she woke, the shadows coming through the windows fell in long slants, and she knew she was late. She also remembered how brash and blunt Gage could be, and it seemed like she'd constantly be at war with herself about the man who'd come suddenly into her life.

She stood, a sigh leaking from her body. A dog barked, and she yelped as her bedroom door wasn't even closed. But that dog bark meant Gage was in her house with Britta.

Sure enough, a moment later, the great big mutt came trotting through the doorway, and Sheryl wanted to bend down and pat her. But she wasn't dressed, so she scampered into her bathroom first, saying, "Just a second, Britta."

Thankfully, she didn't hear Gage at all, and she managed to pull on the appropriate clothing before heading out into the living room. Gage was just sitting up, his eyes still half-closed as he wiped his big hands down his face.

Britta barked again, and he said, "Shush, dog," in a surly tone.

"It's time to get up, sleepyhead," she said as if she herself hadn't just woken up.

"Oh, hey," he said, quickly standing. "I didn't mean to fall asleep. There's just something...comfortable about your place." He flinched. "I mean your house. Your couch. It's a comfortable couch." He patted it as if it were a dog, and Sheryl looked at him, trying to figure out what he was saying.

He cleared his throat. "When do we need to go?" He bent to pick up his phone. "Oh, looks like right now."

"I just need to finish getting ready," she said, though her stick-straight hair would hardly take any time at all and she never wore a lot of makeup. "I just thought I heard Britta, so I came to see if you were here too."

"I'm here too." His eyes met hers, and the moment turned scalding hot.

"What did you have for lunch?" she asked, the words barely making it out of her throat.

"Footlong," he said. "It's one of my favorite foods."

That got her to laugh. "Of course it is. You have the diet of a twelve-year-old boy."

"Hey, it's working well enough so far," he said with a grin, and this was the man Sheryl really liked. The one who smiled and teased and flirted. She liked Gage when he was himself, not Gage when he was a bodyguard.

You should fire him, she told herself. *Ask him out instead.* Startled by the idea, she turned back to her bedroom and said, "I'll be right out." She hurried through her makeup, hair, and jewelry, returning to the living room in under ten minutes.

The back door stood open, and she heard Gage whistle for Britta. They came in together, the dog coming over for a real rub down this time. Sheryl laughed as she ran her hands along the dog's back, as Britta wove between her legs like a cat, nearly knocking her off her feet.

"Britt, come on," Gage said, and the dog trotted over to him. "Can I leave her here?"

"Sure," Sheryl said.

"Let me just get her some water." He started opening cupboards, a panicked look on his face quickly forming.

Sheryl giggled and hipped him out of her kitchen. "I'll get her some water."

"I can do it."

"I'm sure you can." But Sheryl pulled out a big, plastic mixing bowl and filled it with cold water while Gage stood there and watched her. "There you go, Britty baby."

"Oh-ho." Gage chortled, and Sheryl grinned at him.

"Okay," she said. "Let's go. I'll text Javier that we're just leaving."

Gage slipped his hand into hers as they went out the front door, leaving Britta to slurp her water happily in the kitchen. Sheryl got her own helmet latched this time, and the backs of her thighs burned a little against the black leather seat on his motorcycle. But there was nowhere else she'd rather be, so she wrapped her arms around him and said, "Ready."

Twenty minutes later, they pulled up to Javier's house, which was only ten minutes from Sheryl's. "I don't like yelling directions from behind you," she said as she took off her helmet.

"Yeah, that wasn't ideal." He put their helmets in the saddlebag and looked toward the house. "So how are things going tonight?"

"Things?"

"Yeah," he said. "Am I holding your hand? Not holding your hand? How are you going to introduce me?"

Sheryl liked that Gage asked hard questions, seemingly without any embarrassment. She liked the tousled look of his hair, the way he took care of details like watering his dog and stowing the helmets out of sight.

"I don't know yet," she said. "I guess we'll find out."

The front door opened just as she finished talking, and she started walking that way. "Hey, Melinda. Oh, my holy stars in heaven. You look like you're going to pop."

And she so did. Sheryl practically ran up the sidewalk and steps and put her hand on Melinda's elbow, because there was no way the woman could balance as front-heavy as she was. Sheryl had dealt with quite a lot of jealousy over the years as her friends got married one by one, moved on from their single lives, and started families.

The green-eyed monster reared its ugly head again, but she covered over the feelings with a smile. Melinda was older than her, and this was her and Javier's first child. Not everything had to be accomplished by age thirty. And Sheryl wasn't that much older than thirty anyway.

Melinda smiled and said, "I'm so glad you came. Javier acts like I'm going to break."

Sheryl took her hand off Melinda's arm and let her waddle into the house first. She glanced back at Gage, who was just now coming up the steps. One look at his handsome face, and she knew how tonight was going to go.

She put her hand in his and went in the house after Melinda, the air conditioning delicious on this hot, humid South Carolina night. "Mel, this is my boyfriend, Gage."

"Boyfriend?" Javier called, darting out from behind the wall that separated part of the kitchen from the living room. He laughed as he wiped his hands on a kitchen towel and tossed it on the counter. "I knew it.

Sheryl." He shook his head and came into the living room. "You're a sneaky one." He shook Gage's hand. "I'm Javier Garcia."

"Javier," Sheryl said, her voice a little tight. "He's worked at the inn forever."

"Forever?" Javier scoffed. "Nope. But a while. This is my wife, Melinda."

"Gage Sanders," Sheryl said before Gage had to introduce himself. "Javvy says you've worked for his family's water park a couple of times."

"Oh, of course," Gage said, polished and perfect—exactly the man Sheryl had dreamt about. "Riverdale, right?"

"Right." Javier beamed at Gage. "My father runs the place."

"Good concerts there," Gage said. "Tell him I'm available any time." He glanced at Sheryl, his hand tightening in hers. "Except for the surfing competition. I'm working that."

"Oh, he knows better than to schedule something against the surfing," Javier said. "Come in, come in. You don't have to hover by the front door." He moved back into the kitchen, Melinda following him.

Sheryl went before Gage, glad she'd gotten an awkward introduction out of the way. "Holy cow, Mel." She took in the spread of food in front of her. "I told Gage you would do this, but it's still a little overwhelming."

"Oh, it's just tacos," she said.

"Just tacos?" Gage had joined Sheryl. "This looks amazing."

Melinda had prepared authentic refried beans, Spanish rice, fresh tortillas that Sheryl had seen her hand-roll in the past, and all the toppings. Little bowls held cheese, lettuce, olives, tomatoes, salsa, and a variety of sauces.

"Which one is the spiciest?" Sheryl asked, reaching for a handful of chips.

"The red one," Javier said. "The green one is more mild."

"I'm starving," Mel said, and Gage added, "Me too."

"Oh, he's always starving," Sheryl teased, glad when Gage's dark eyes sparkled instead of turning hard.

"Hey, that footlong was hours ago," he said. "And I forgot to tell you my brother is coming into town tomorrow."

"Oh?" Sheryl took the plate Javier handed her, but she didn't immediately dive into assembling her taco. "You can have the day off, if you want."

"Day off?" Mel asked at the same time Gage said, "That's not necessary."

Sheryl looked back and forth between Mel and Gage. "Uh, Gage is sort of my bodyguard too."

"Bodyguard with benefits, babe," Javier said, throwing a teasing look at Sheryl. She rolled her eyes and started making her tacos as Mel nodded.

Melinda and Javier cleared out of the kitchen, and

Gage moved around to the other side of the counter to spoon beans and rice onto his plate. "Is that true?" he asked, not looking up from his food.

"Which part?"

"Bodyguard with benefits?" He looked at her then, and Sheryl shrugged.

"I guess we'll see."

He chuckled and shook his head, finished piling chips on his plate, and joined her friends at their dining room table. "Oh, hello there," he said to their pup, and Sheryl took a few extra moments in the kitchen to spoon on a healthy amount of sour cream. Mel bought it for her, she knew, and she also knew the green sauce would exceed her spice level, so a lot of sour cream was needed.

She watched Gage for as long as she dared, and he certainly seemed at ease folding over his taco and lifting it to his lips.

Heat shot through Sheryl as she watched that mouth, wondering what it would feel like against hers when the kiss was real.

"That was amazing," Gage said as they stood at his motorcycle, fastening their helmet straps.

"They're great," Sheryl said.

"*You're* great," Gage said, swinging his leg over his bike. Sheryl paused, sure she hadn't heard him right.

Why wouldn't you have heard him right? she thought.

"Thanks," she said. "You're not so bad yourself."

"You think so?" He started the bike in the next moment, and she climbed on behind him, the seat just as hot now as it had been earlier, though the sun had gone down.

"I do," she said. "You just have a loud bark sometimes."

"I don't mean to," he said, turning his head so she could hear him better. "And how big of a hurry are you in to get home?"

"I'm not the one who just said we needed to leave so he could let his dog out."

He chuckled, and Sheryl held onto him, the strength in his back comforting and sexy at the same time. He took them away from her house, winding along until he got to the coastal highway. They'd driven this road together before, but it was different at night.

More magical. More beautiful. More romantic.

She adored riding on the back of this motorcycle with this man, and she decided she was going to kiss him before he left that night. Somehow.

Nerves fluttered in her chest. It had been a long time since she'd kissed a man. Since she'd opened herself up to anyone new, really.

He took them back to her place, parked in his spot, and they went into the house together. He did step over to the back door to let Britta out while Sheryl picked up the mixing bowl and started washing it.

"Go on," she heard him say to the dog, and Britta came back inside, followed by Gage. He swept his arm around her waist and pressed a kiss to her temple. "I'm going to head out. Early day tomorrow."

"Early day every day," she said, leaning into his touch as a bright light of happiness moved through her.

"Mm." He stepped back and walked away, sending her heartbeat crashing around inside her chest like cymbals. He wouldn't just leave. Would he?

He would, and he was.

Sheryl tossed the sponge back in the sink as he said, "Come on, Brit. I'll go slower than I did this afternoon."

"Hey, yeah," she said, though it was practically a yell. Gage turned back to her, his eyes widening with surprise. "How did you get her here on the bike?"

He bent down and clipped a leash to his dog's collar. "She ran. I rode." He gave her another grin and turned again.

Sheryl didn't quite know what to do. She darted around the couch and met him at the door. "Thanks for coming with me tonight."

"It was really fun," he said. "I don't get out socially, if you know what I mean."

Oh, she did.

Without second guessing or saying anything else, she tipped up onto her toes and said, "I don't want you to leave without kissing me."

Gage searched her face, not a smile in sight. Sheryl wasn't smiling either, because she was dead serious.

"Bodyguard with benefits," he said, lowering his mouth to hers. And wow, Sheryl could barely stand with the taste, the touch, the towering presence of this man.

10

Gage could kiss Sheryl forever. This kiss was different than the one he'd laid on her on her doorstep days ago.

How many days, he wasn't sure.

He wasn't sure of anything in that moment. Only kissing Sheryl mattered. He growled as her fingernails moved up his scalp and into his hair. He turned her so she was pressed into her front door, and he kissed her like he was starving for something only she could provide.

She matched every stroke of his mouth, and he dropped his lips to her neck. "Gage," she whispered, only encouraging him.

He could not get enough of her skin, her perfume, her lips. He kissed her again, slowing down now so he could really take his time, commit this kiss to memory. By the time he pulled away, he felt like his lips would be bruised come morning, and everyone would know what he'd been doing.

He sighed, the only visceral response his body had for this woman. She was beautiful, and kind, and forgiving, and he liked her far more than he'd thought he was capable of.

"I should go," he said, his voice froggy and throaty and hardly his own.

"Yeah," she said. But she didn't move so he could open the front door and go. Their eyes met, and they smiled simultaneously.

"All right," she said, stepping sideways and reaching up to smooth her hair where he'd messed it up. "Yeah. Okay. You should go."

"I'll see you tomorrow," he said, forcing himself to open the door instead of kissing her again. The air outside was still hot, but it was infinitely cooler than the climate inside her beach cottage. He took in a deep breath and slowed Britta as the dog tried to bolt down the steps. He turned back to see Sheryl had grabbed onto the door, as if she couldn't stand by herself. "Bye."

"Bye," she repeated, a blissful look in her eyes. She brought the door closed, and Gage went down the steps, happier than he'd been in a long, long time.

"She's great, right?" he asked Britta as he tied the leash to his handlebars. "Makes you wonder why she likes me." He glanced back up to the door, but Sheryl hadn't come out.

He did have a loud bark sometimes, and sometimes it served him well. It kept him employed, for one. But he could work on being softer with Sheryl if it would earn him another kiss like that one.

THE NEXT DAY AFTER WORK, GAGE PULLED INTO HIS driveway to find the front door open. He stared at it as he got off his motorcycle, trying to be as silent as possible. If the door was open, Britta would be gone, as she didn't need a reason to run toward the rectangle of light.

He kept his helmet under his arm as he approached the house. He pulled his phone out of his pocket and typed in nine-one-one, but he didn't dial it yet. "Hello?" he called as he went up the steps.

A dog barked in the distance, and it sounded suspiciously like Britta.

Gage stepped inside and saw a couple of pieces of luggage by the door, and everything came back to him. The Army green duffle bag definitely belonged to his brother, and he'd probably just forgotten to make sure the door had latched behind him.

Gage hadn't told him to check on that, and the wind on the beach had a reputation of pulling on unlatched doors and opening them.

A moment later, Britta barked again, this time jumping up the back steps and galloping into the house.

"Oh, hey," he said, laughing. "There you are. Is Uncle Mike here? Is he? Is he throwing you a ball?"

He scrubbed the sand out of Britta's wet beard, not even caring that the floor was getting dirty and slobbery. His brother filled the doorway, and Gage straightened, a smile on his face. "Hey." He laughed again as he embraced Michael, and it was good to see his brother. Have a human connection.

"How are you?"

"I've been better," he said, stepping back, the smile still stuck on his face. Pain lived in his eyes, but he smothered it quickly and looked around the small beach house. "This place is great. Right on the water."

"Yeah," Gage said. "Listen, I didn't tell you this, but I kind of have another job this afternoon. Every afternoon, actually."

"You're working two jobs?"

"Whatever it takes to pay the bills," he said, though he didn't technically need Sheryl's money. He liked being busy, and he liked saving money for a rainy day. He wanted to live on his ferry income and the extra jobs he picked up. His Marine pension went into a bank account every month, and he was determined to keep it that way.

"How's Mom?" Gage asked, stepping over to the fridge and pulling out a package of deli ham. "And you're welcome to come with me this afternoon. I texted my... girlfriend, and she says it's fine."

Michael blinked. "Let me back up a minute." He shook

his head as if to align the thoughts. "You work for your girlfriend?"

"It's a complicated situation," Gage admitted. "And the girlfriend part is still new." He hoped his brother would get the message, and he seemed to.

"Great. But I don't need to tag along."

"I already talked to her," Gage said. "We're meeting at the bakery at the inn where she works. They have sandwiches and stuff like that. Then I just take her home and hang out."

"Is that some sort of freaky code I don't know because I'm married?" Michael asked.

Gage blinked and then burst out laughing. "No, bro. Nothing like that. I'm her bodyguard. She has a bit of a stalker problem, and I literally babysit her in the afternoon and evening so she feels safe."

"But she's your girlfriend." Michael raised his eyebrows.

"I mean, it's new," Gage said. "Maybe you could just come to lunch and then we'll see how things go."

"I'm down with that," Michael said. "And Mom's doing okay." He sighed, which meant she wasn't doing great. But honestly, Gage hadn't returned to Peach Tree, because their mother was never doing very well.

She was either on the edge of going to rehab or just getting out, and nothing Gage or Michael had done over the years had seemed to make a difference.

"How'd you get here?" he asked.

"Pedicab. Do you actually drive the car out there?" He hooked his thumb over his shoulder, toward the front of the house.

"Not for a while," Gage said, opening a drawer and rummaging around until he found the key. "See if you can start it."

Michael grinned, took the key, and headed outside. Gage checked on Britta's food and water, and gave her another pat. "I'll send Ginger to take you out tonight, okay, girl?" He hurried to text the teen who sometimes came to take care of his dog and went outside just as the car's engine roared to life.

"Follow me," he said, putting his helmet back on. "It's at The Heartwood Inn, and I park around the back, in case you get lost."

Michael waved at him, and Gage took off for the inn. His brother coming to the island hadn't happened at a great time, but he couldn't change it. His brother could take care of himself while Gage worked, because starting tomorrow, he was about to have three jobs.

After they'd parked and were walking in together, Gage asked, "So you probably don't want to talk about it, but what happened with Marie?"

"I was overseas a lot," he said, as if that summed it all up.

Gage didn't think it did. "Yeah, so are a lot of men and women."

"She says I missed too much, that she doesn't need me, because I'm never around anyway."

Gage stopped, though it was much too hot to linger outside in this bright sunshine. "Wow, Mike. That's...hurtful."

His brother nodded and shrugged. "She said she needs some time, and I didn't know how to argue against that." He sighed and looked out toward the beach. "Honestly, I couldn't fight with her anymore."

Gage clapped him on the shoulder and said, "All right. Well, I'm glad you're here. I'll be working security at this beach next week for the surfing championship. So you'll be pretty good friends with Britta this week." He opened the door to the bakery and spotted Sheryl instantly.

"Do you think your girlfriend would hire me?" Michael asked, and Gage looked at him.

"I don't know. Let's ask her." He nodded toward the beautiful blonde who had her hand in the air as if he wasn't drawn to her the moment he saw her. He crossed the bakery to her, effortlessly weaving through tables to find she already had their food in front of her.

"Hey," he said, taking her into his arms and hugging her for a moment. He wanted to hold on for a lot longer, but he didn't want to cause a scene. "This is my brother, Michael. Michael, my girlfriend, Sheryl."

It felt so good to say those words and have her beam at his brother like she was pleased as punch to meet him. Of course, she probably was. Sheryl seemed to have a lot of friends, and she could talk to anyone.

"I got our sandwiches already," she said. "Sit down."

Gage sat by her and let Michael take one of the chairs across from them. "He's wondering about a job."

"Are you serious?" Her eyes lit up. "Because I just had two guys say they couldn't rake the beach tomorrow, and I'll take anything with two hands. Flippers, even."

Michael said, "I'm in," and Sheryl started laughing.

"You should hear what I'm going to do to you before you accept," she said, leaning forward. "There's a reason two guys quit last minute." She giggled again, and Gage basked in the sound of it, feeling happier than he had in a long time. He slipped his arm around her waist, and she leaned into him next, and he thought he might actually have a chance of falling in love with this woman.

His pulse stumbled around like the intoxicated man he'd removed from the ferry that morning. He'd never been an overly emotional guy. Never really considered himself capable of carving a spot for someone else in his life.

But a very Sheryl-sized hole was burrowing into his heart, and he couldn't do anything to stop it.

11

*S*heryl stood under the umbrella she'd set up first thing that morning, almost before the sun had gotten up. Well, that was practically impossible unless she got up as early as her sister Alissa did. She was out on *Big Blue* by three each morning to get the fish the chefs needed for the restaurant at the inn.

She looked at her clipboard and said, "Javier, we need the grandstands to run the entire length of the beach. Where are the rest of them?"

"That's all we've got," he said.

Sheryl frowned out at the half-dozen men making sure the stands would stay put in the sand. "That can't be right. There are only six of them. I know we have eight."

"I thought we did too," he said, lifting a water bottle to his lips. She'd lectured everyone at six-thirty that morning to drink enough. Come stand in the shade if they got overheated. Eat something. She had food and water on-hand, and she'd ordered all the ice cream from the grocery store last night for their end-of-setup banana split party.

The grocery store here on the island made specialty ice creams, including a banana pudding one that was killer with more bananas, hot fudge and caramel sauce. Her mouth watered just thinking about it.

"I'm going to go check the shed," she said.

"Simon was already in there this morning."

"I know we have more stands." She handed him the clipboard. "Keep them working. Garbage cans are next, and Helen is bringing those in. She'll be here in five minutes."

Sheryl hated walking through sand in sneakers, but she couldn't show up for work in her swimming suit and flip flops. So she wore her uniform, complete with the white sneakers to show solidarity with her grounds crew. She straddled the ATV and started toward the southwest side of the inn. The tennis courts were over here, along with that stretch of sidewalk with the flower beds she'd re-barked.

They also had a huge storage shed behind a tall fence, and she left the ATV running while she jumped down to unlock the gate with her keycard. An electronic record of every entry and exit was kept on the inn's computer system, and she could check to see if Simon had indeed been there that morning.

But she didn't need to. Simon was trustworthy, and

he'd definitely gotten the stands out that morning. Her ATV didn't have a wagon or trailer attached, and she wasn't sure how she'd get the stands back even if she found them.

"Call someone," she told herself as she motored over to the biggest door on the side of the shed. It went up with screeches and groans, and sure enough, there were no more stands inside.

Olympia would lose her mind if Sheryl told her they were short twenty-five-percent of their seating. Her sister sold tickets for those seats, and they cost more than just a spot of sand on the beach. They needed those stands.

"Missing something?" a man asked, and Sheryl spun around, her heart ricocheting around inside her chest.

"Ricky." She backed up a step, pressing one hand to her rapid-fire pulse while her other went immediately to her phone. "How did you get in here?"

"That's not important."

Of course it was important, but Sheryl didn't want to argue with him. "You told Gage you'd stay away."

"Did I?" He took a step forward, and she went backward again, realizing that she was moving into the empty storage shed. "I don't remember doing that."

"I'm calling the police," she said, glancing down at her phone for just a moment. But in that breath of time, Ricky had gotten closer. Too close. She looked right into his eyes, and pure fear seeped into her very bones.

"I'm not going to hurt you," he said, though his eyes

sparked with a type of danger that said otherwise. "Sheryl, I need a job. I know you're doing the beach for the surfing championship, and I'll do whatever it takes to get on the crew." He didn't look away from her, and her compassion swam through her.

"Where are the stands?"

"I'm sure I can help you find them." He lifted his chin. "If you hire me on."

Sheryl didn't see how she could. But she also needed those grandstands, and she knew Ricky had taken them and knew right where they were. Indecision raged through her as she tried to find another solution.

"Sheryl," he said.

"Fine," she snapped at him. "You don't talk to me. You'll get all of your assignments from Javier, and you won't talk to anyone else either. Are we clear?"

"Yes, ma'am."

"This is a temporary job. One week. If you're late, even one minute late, you're fired."

"I won't be late."

"If I see you talking to someone, and I don't like it, you're out of here."

"Fine."

Sheryl tried to think of anything else she needed to have on the list of things he couldn't do. "You won't ask me for a permanent job when this is done."

"Okay."

"And you will apologize for taking my grandstands so you could pull this little stunt."

"I'm sorry," he said. "I'm just desperate. My mom isn't well."

Sheryl's heart bled a little bit more for him, but she refused to show it. Gage would be so proud.

A silent groan started in her stomach. Gage. He'd be livid when he learned about Ricky stealing her grandstands and then getting a job out of it. He'd probably come supervise the activities on the beach just to make sure Ricky behaved.

"Okay," she said. "Take me to my grandstands." She could deal with Gage later. Right now, she had an entire beach to set up for the surfing championship, an event that brought a lot of people and a lot of money to the inn.

By the next afternoon, they had the viewing area set up and roped off. Now she needed to get the kiosks set up—first aid, water, extra restrooms, and merchandizing. She'd told Gage he should spend the afternoon with his brother, because she would be going to visit her parents and grandmother, and three o'clock found her stumbling up their front steps, the heat from the sun almost too much to bear.

"Hey," she called as she entered. "It's just me. I come bearing afternoon biscuits for your tea." How her mother and grandmother drank tea in the summer, Sheryl wasn't sure. It seemed obscene to her, and yet, every Thursday afternoon, they pretended to be English royalty.

"Hello, dear," her mother said, getting up from the table to give Sheryl a hug. "Where's your bodyguard?"

"I gave him the day off," she said, deciding on the spot not to tell them that Gage had graduated to boyfriend status. "I figured you guys could babysit me just as easily." She set down the box of cookies Alissa had put together that morning. "Where's Dad?"

"He went over to Celeste's. I guess she's got a leak in her bathroom."

Sheryl nodded, because their dad was constantly helping one of them. Or fishing. He liked to do that too. "No rummy today?"

"Grandma's into cribbage lately," her mom said. "Right, Mom?"

"Want to play?" she asked Sheryl.

She looked at the board with the pegs. "It's been too long. I'll just watch." Then she could text Gage if she wanted to. Field questions from Javier or Simon. And maybe doze a little bit.

"How are the preparations for the surfing championship going?" her mom asked.

"Tiring," Sheryl said. "I swear, I love my job fifty-one weeks out of the year. This is the week I don't." She sighed as she sat at the dining room table too. This had been the same table where she'd grown up eating dinner, all of her sisters there every night. Her dad would even come home from the inn and spend an hour with them, sometimes going back to work or straight to bed.

But she'd never doubted that her parents loved her. They'd provided a good life for her and her sisters, and she was grateful she could still see them every day if she wanted to.

Their house had not been big, and all five girls had shared a bathroom. When her mother needed space, she stayed in a room at the inn—at least in the winter months. During the summer, The Heartwood Inn was constantly booked.

Her phone chimed, and she glanced at Gage's text. Did you make it? You said you were going to text me.

Half-appreciation, half-annoyance filled her, and she quickly tapped out, *Made it,* so he'd leave her alone. She couldn't really be upset though. He had asked her to text him when she got to her mother's, and she'd said she would.

"We're thinking about getting a cat," her mom said, and Sheryl whipped her head away from her phone.

"What? Dad's allergic to cats."

"At least you heard me," her mom said, picking up another card. "I've been talking to myself for five minutes."

"Sorry, someone texted."

"Yeah, Gage," Grandma said. "I saw the message." She

was like Double-Oh-Granny, and Sheryl swept her phone off the table and into her lap.

"How did you even see that?" she asked.

"Granny has new glasses," she said proudly. "Plus, Doris down at the salon told me you two are dating. Is that true?"

"Dating?" Her mom's shriek practically took the roof off of the house. "Sheryl?" She wore so much hope in her eyes that Sheryl would've said yes even if it wasn't true.

"Mom, this is not a big deal. I mean, Olympia's dating that guy across the hall from her. Alissa's back with Shawn. Can we not make this like an event of the century?"

"It's just that you haven't dated anyone for so long."

"Thanks for reminding me." She rolled her eyes, regretting the afternoon already, and she'd been there for ten minutes.

"So tell us about him," her mom prompted.

"You met him, Mom."

"I know, I know," she said, laying down her cards and moving her peg. "But tell us all the juicy stuff."

"Oh, you want the tea."

"No," her grandmother said, leaning closer as if Sheryl hadn't heard her. "We want to know how things are going with Gage." She looked at Sheryl's mother. "But I suppose we could have tea and biscuits with it."

"Now's a good time to break," her mom said, getting up from the table again. "I'll get the cups."

"I'll get the cookies," her grandmother said.

And that left the tea to Sheryl. And not just the kind that could be poured from a pot. She sighed as she set the kettle to boil and pulled the teabags from the cupboard. She wasn't even sure where to begin with Gage. He was a complicated man, though he seemed simple on the outside.

Her phone chimed again, but she'd left it over on the table. So her grandmother picked up the device and read, "Okay, sorry. I didn't mean to bark so loud." She looked perplexed as she studied the phone. "What does that mean?"

"Nothing," Sheryl said, a smile forming on her face and moving through her soul. "Gage can be a bit demanding sometimes, that's all." And that was the tip of the iceberg. But he was her iceberg, and Sheryl just needed to figure out a way to keep chipping away at him until he melted completely.

With a jolt, she realized she was thinking of changing him. As if she could really do that. She knew she couldn't; she'd already ruined one relationship with her attempts to form Chuck into the man she wished he was instead of being satisfied with the person he already was.

She frowned at herself and then the teapot as it began to whistle. How long had she been standing there, thinking about Gage?

Too long.

She pulled the kettle from the burner and poured the

hot water over the teabags her mom had lovingly laid in the cups. "Mom," she said, catching her mom mid-bite on a chocolate chip oatmeal cookie. She forged on anyway. "How did you know you could spend your whole life with Dad and not go crazy?"

Her mom choked, tried to swallow, and ended up spraying cookie crumbs out of her mouth. Her laughter followed, but Sheryl didn't know what she'd said that was so funny.

When her mom finally quieted, she picked up her napkin and started wiping up the crumbs. "Oh, honey. I never felt that way. He drives me crazy to this day. You just learn to compromise."

"Compromise," Sheryl said. So she could forgive Gage his bark, and he'd forgive her super sensitivity to his bark. Or something.

"The tea is getting cold," Grandma said, and Sheryl refrained from rolling her eyes. It was hard, but she did it. Just like it was hard not to be annoyed whenever Gage texted her. But she could do it.

I hope, she thought. She did like Gage. She just didn't like every single thing about him. But as far as flaws went, sending curt texts probably wasn't that big of a deal.

Was it?

12

Gage growled as he pressed Sheryl into the metal door of her office, easily turning the deadbolt as he did. The last thing he needed was one of her crew members coming in while he made out with her. Or for his brother to stumble upon them, as he happened to work for Sheryl now.

"Gage," she said breathlessly, and he took the opportunity to move his mouth to her neck. She tasted like sweat and sunscreen, and he was ravenous for more of her. He hadn't seen her as much since she'd started making preparations for the surfing competition several days ago. Once it started, he'd be working long afternoons in the sun. It would be another nine days before they got back to their normal schedule and sneaking into her office with her for a few minutes had become their new "normal" for the last few days.

She ran her fingernails through his hair and giggled, the sound like the sweetest song in Gage's ears. He pulled back with some difficulty, his breathing ragged to match the marching of his pulse.

"I haven't seen you in forever," he said, his voice rough around the edges.

"It was last night," she said, smiling as she pressed her lips to his again in a chaste kiss.

"Feels like a long time." With his head clearer, he stepped away from her fully and said, "I brought that turkey bacon wrap you like for lunch." She'd been working longer hours, the only thing keeping her going was some banana split party on the horizon.

She'd invited him to it as well, and he'd said he'd come. He just wanted to spend time with Sheryl, learn all about her that he could. He'd been working with her for just over a week, but it felt like a lot longer.

"Thanks," she said.

"How are things going with the new stuff Olympia is doing?" he asked. "Oh, and that hammock is at your place. I'll go over this afternoon with Britta and put it up for you, if you want."

"I definitely want you to do that," she said, rounding her desk and sitting down. She pulled the white deli bag toward her and looked inside. "And Olympia's, well, Olympia. She's constantly trying to think of things to make Heartwood better. She's been going nuts training new staff for actual food service during the surfing competition. We've never done that before."

"It's a good idea." Gage pulled out the folding chair and sat down across from her.

"Did you eat already?" she asked, taking out her wrap.

"No, mine is in there," he said. She reached in again and pulled out another sandwich.

"Oh, it sure is." She looked at it. "California club? Really? That has sprouts and stuff on it." She made a face, which made Gage want to kiss her again.

"Yeah." He took it from her and started unwrapping it. "It's good."

"I don't like roast beef on a sandwich."

"You've told me," he said. "So, tell me something I don't know. Where would you go on vacation if you could go anywhere?"

"Anywhere?" Her eyebrows went up.

"Anywhere."

"Iceland," she said. "To see the Northern Lights."

He nodded, a smile touching his mouth. He took a bite of his sandwich, expecting the same question in return. They'd been doing this during lunchtime for the past few days, and that was how he'd learned she didn't like roast beef on sandwiches. And that she loved watching crime dramas on TV, and that she always had sour candy in her purse.

He'd told her more about himself than anyone else in

the past few years, and when he'd realized that, he'd felt kind of stupid. But he'd never needed a lot of friends or people around him. In fact, while he loved having the island bursting with tourists, he also liked the smaller crowd of locals that hung around in the winter too.

"And you?" she asked.

"Maybe England?"

"You're guessing?" she teased.

"Well, I've been a few places with the Marines," he said. "The Middle East. Hawaii. Africa." He shrugged like it was no big deal, because it wasn't. He certainly hadn't taken any safaris or surfing lessons while on active duty. "But I've never been to England, and I think it would be fun."

"We should go," she said, a genuine smile on her face.

Gage nodded, because he didn't know what else to do. "Do you actually take time off work?"

She laughed as she shook her head. "No. Do you?"

"Hardly ever." He grinned at her and took another bite of his sandwich. He loved being with her like this, eating and talking. It was simple, sure. Comforting. He felt himself slip a little bit, and he knew he was very close to falling in love with this woman.

It seemed impossible that he could be so close after only several days. They had spent a lot of time together, and while they didn't always get along, they always made up.

"Favorite junk food," she said.

"I have to pick one?"

"Top three."

"Pizza," he said.

"That's not a junk food," she argued. "It has like four food groups."

"Sure, okay." He laughed. "Popcorn from the theater, with a lot of butter." He waited for her to say something, but she didn't. So he continued with, "Corndogs and French fries."

She finished chewing, her eyes bright and blue and beautiful. "You just named all my favorite things."

"Yeah? You can't add to the top three?"

"For the record, you named four things." She gave him a *so-there* look, and then tossed her ponytail over her shoulder. "Soda, popcorn with a lot of butter, and...." She cocked her head as if she were really thinking hard about it.

Gage found her to be the most attractive creature he'd ever laid eyes on, and he couldn't help chuckling as he finished his sandwich.

"Candy."

"That's a huge category," he said. "And so is soda. I think you might be cheating."

"Can we cheat at this game?" She wiped her hands on her napkins, her face full of flirt.

"Nope." Gage got up and collected their trash. "All

right. I'm going to go get Britta and get that hammock done." He leaned down to kiss her, and she tilted her head back to receive it. All the fun, flirtiness from their conversation fled as she poured passion into her kiss.

Gage held her face in his hands, breathless from the first moment she touched him. He could kiss her all afternoon and still not be satisfied.

Someone knocked on her door and tried to open it, effectively making Gage jump away from her as if he'd been caught doing something wrong.

"Just a sec," Sheryl called, straightening the collar on her polo as she stood. "Go on, you," she whispered. "You're going to get me in trouble."

"With who?" he asked, genuinely wanting to know, as he moved toward the door. He flipped the deadbolt and opened the door, coming face to face with not just one, but two of Sheryl's sisters.

Olympia he'd met at the bonfire. The other blonde had to be Celeste, as she worked for the inn doing special events and wedding planning, and she wore a cute pencil skirt with a tight-fitting blouse. He didn't think a chef or a shrimp boat captain—what Gwen and Alissa did for a living—would wear such things to work.

"Hey," he said. "Hello."

"Gage," Sheryl said. "You know my sisters, Olympia and Celeste."

"Of course." He saluted for a reason he couldn't name and said, "See you later, Sheryl."

Both Olympia and Celeste backed out of the doorway so Gage could squeeze by them, neither of them removing their eyes from him. He smiled and headed for the outdoor exit, feeling the weight of their gazes on him the whole time.

"Come on," Sheryl said behind him. "Stop staring."

"What were you two doing in there?" Olympia asked, obviously not trying to keep her voice down. "The door was locked."

"I've never even seen this door closed," Celeste said.

Sheryl laughed, and it took everything inside Gage not to turn around and wave good-bye to her. He made it out of the building without incident, taking a big breath of the hot, sea air outside.

"Okay," he told himself, not checking for Ricky's truck or anyone lurking nearby. "Time to put a hammock in a tree."

Because if he did that, then he could hold Sheryl in his arms as the sun went down. Kiss her as the night stole the life from the day and they swayed back and forth in the breeze. Maybe murmur to her that he was falling in love with her.

Maybe.

SHE FINISHED THE PREPARATIONS FOR THE SURFING competition, and Gage started his training for the security at the surfing competition. Nine days became eight, became seven, and it was time for the banana split party.

"Okay," she said, pushing a cart full of bananas toward the back of the grocery store. "Now we just need the ice cream, and we can go."

He pushed a cart too, this one laden with cans of fake whipped cream, jars of hot fudge and caramel sauce, and bags of chopped peanuts. He also had the bowls, spoons, and napkins, and they'd been in the store for entirely too long.

But the surfing competition started tomorrow morning, and Gage would be working security on the sand for the next eight afternoons. Olympia had hired more men than just him, and his evenings would be free to spend with Sheryl and that new hammock he'd put in the tree in her backyard.

They hadn't been able to use it quite yet, and he was really looking forward to it.

"Hey," she said to the guy at the butcher counter. "I have an order for thirty gallons of ice cream. Half banana and half vanilla."

"Let me check for you." The man turned and went through the swinging door that led into the back.

"This is the butcher counter," Gage said.

"Yeah, this is where you pick up special orders from the dairy department." She looked at him, her eyes sparkling. "You were worried."

"It's the butcher counter," he said again. But a few

moments later, the man returned with three other people, all of them carrying huge buckets of ice cream.

"Ah, thanks," Sheryl said, beaming at them. After a few adjustments were made, they got the buckets in their carts and headed to the check-out.

Over at the inn, he worked to get everything set up for the party. He put up tables and chairs while she set out bowls and spoons and all the toppings. Before long, everyone on the grounds crew came inside most of them smelling like sunscreen, salt, and sweat.

"All right," Sheryl said loudly, and everyone quieted down. She smiled around at them, and a rush of pride moved through Gage to watch her take control over the group. She was smart, and strong, and sexy, and he couldn't wait to be alone with her again.

"Thank you all for working so hard this year," she said. "The beach looks beautiful, and we got everything done on time, despite a few hiccups and new demands. It's our annual banana split party." She gestured to the tables. "But first, I have some bonuses to hand out." She took a few steps over to the table and picked up a stack of envelopes.

"For solving problems with a smile." She looked out at the group. "Simon Smith."

Everyone clapped, and Gage felt their sense of unity, their sense of family, of belonging. And he knew who had established and cultivated that. Sheryl.

She continued with the awards, and then said, "All right. Time to feast!"

Chatter erupted as people got up and started scooping ice cream and spooning on hot fudge. Gage enjoyed himself, talking to a few people he'd seen around—especially Javier. He liked ice cream almost as well as corndogs or the footlongs from the vendor down at South Port, and he ate three bowls before kissing Sheryl and saying, "See you in a bit."

He had to go to one more meeting with Olympia, and then he'd take Sheryl home. He had something special planned for them that night, and he couldn't wait to be alone with her.

The meeting was long, and boring, and nothing he didn't already know. By the time he made it back downstairs to her office, the tables and chairs and leftovers had been cleaned up. His footsteps echoed off the cement in the silence, and he stepped over to Sheryl's office.

He froze, his heartbeat booming in his chest, his throat, his ears.

There had been a struggle in this office. Sheryl always left everything in its exact-right spot, and she would never leave several folders worth of papers strewn on the floor. Or her laptop open and unsecured. Or her soda sitting on the desk.

Gage spun away from the crime scene, reaching for his phone. He dialed Sheryl first, and her phone rang in the office behind him.

Definitely a problem. She never went anywhere without her phone. Ever.

His next call went to 9-1-1, and he stayed very still and out of the office, just in case there was a clue as to who had taken her or where she'd gone.

13

Sheryl banged on the divider between the back of the van where she currently was and the front, where the driver's seat was. "Let me out of here!" When she'd first been taken from her office, she wasn't sure if she should fight back or go willingly.

But the crime dramas she liked so much had taught her to never get in a car with someone if she could help it. But the burly men who'd come for her hadn't given her a choice. She'd asked them who they were and what they wanted, but neither of them had answered. They'd shoved her in the back of this van, where there were no seats and the windows were painted black, and got in the two front seats.

She'd tried the doors on the side and found them locked with no inside door handles. Same for the back door.

So she'd decided to yell—not that it was doing anything.

She knew she couldn't get off the island without getting on a boat somehow, either a ferry, a sailboat, a yacht, something, and that hadn't happened. So she was still somewhere on Carter's Cove.

She'd made peace with Ricky. At least she thought she had. He'd been working for her on the beach for a few days now. He'd skipped the banana split party, as she'd asked him to, and everything was fine.

She'd just finished cleaning up from that shindig and had sat down at her computer to put in the receipts for it. Olympia had strict policies about that, and Sheryl didn't want to get shut down on her budget by not following the rules.

The outside door had opened, and she'd expected Javier or Gage to darken her doorway. It hadn't been either of them, and Sheryl hadn't even really gotten a good look at either man before they were on top of her, grabbing her arms and hauling her out of her office.

She didn't have her phone, and she was pretty sure she'd knocked several things off her desk as she'd been ripped from the safety of the inn.

How long had gone by?

She pounded on the divider again, using both fists. Her family had had some trouble a couple of weeks ago, getting accused of some graffiti in the high-rise going up just down the street from The Heartwood Inn.

Could this have something to do with that? She'd thought Alissa's boyfriend's co-worker had done it, trying to frame the Heartwoods. Sheryl had thought that was all settled. And if there was someone to take for a ransom, it was Olympia, not her.

"Hey!" she yelled again, and miraculously, a partition slid open, revealing a small window into the front of the van.

"Look," one of the men said, his face filling the window. "We're not—"

She punched him as hard as she could, pain exploding through her knuckles and up her arm. "Let me out of here right this moment," she said.

The man yelped and clutched his face with both hands, a string of expletives coming from his mouth. Sheryl didn't want to get too close lest she get punched too, but she leaned forward and looked at the man driving.

"Get me out of here," she said, trying to infuse as much anger and danger into her voice as she could. "So help me, I'm going to—"

"We're not going to hurt you, Sheryl," he said, glancing at her. "Look, we're at your house." He made a turn, and sure enough, he'd pulled into her driveway.

Confused and completely stumped, Sheryl remained silent.

"We need your help to surprise Gage," the other one

said, dabbing at his nose, where a thin trickle of blood trailed out.

"What?" She had no idea what to say. Surprise Gage? Why?

"He didn't tell you, did he?" the nose-bleeder asked.

"Tell me what? And who *are* you guys?" Gage hadn't told her anything, and he was going to get an earful from Sheryl about it. These two muscled men had *grabbed her from her office.*

All at once, several pieces fell into place. "You're Marines," she said.

"I'm Teddy," the driver said. "And he's Rudy. We served with Gage right up until his retirement." He looked at her quizzically. "He never said anything?"

"And it's his birthday today," Rudy said, glancing at Teddy. "I bet he didn't mention that either."

"Classic Gage," Teddy said with a small smile. "But we heard about you, and we thought you could help us get Gage real good."

"He's mentioned his time in the Marines very little," she said, wishing she'd asked more. But really, she and Gage had only known each other for ten days, and surely she didn't have to know everything about him already. "And no, he never said anything about his birthday."

Her annoyance surged again, and now that she knew she wasn't in any danger, it had plenty of room to bloom and grow. "He's going to get an earful, let me tell you." She patted her back pocket for her phone, remembering she didn't have it.

"Oh, he'll be panicked soon enough," Teddy said. "When he sees your office and you gone...." He burst out laughing, but Sheryl honestly didn't see how this was a funny joke.

"Won't he be upset?"

"That's the point," Rudy said, opening the front door of the van. "He did this to our CO once, and he thought it was funny then."

"Gage doesn't seem like the type to think having the tables turned on him is very funny," Sheryl said, confident that she knew that much.

"Oh, he's not." Teddy got out too, and a moment later, Rudy opened the back door of the van.

Sheryl just looked at him. "Where did you get this vehicle?"

"It belongs to my brother. It's usually full of band equipment. That's why there are tie-downs here." He indicated a divot in the floor Sheryl hadn't even seen.

"I'm calling Gage right now," Teddy said, appearing at the back of the van. Sheryl scooted toward the opening and let Rudy help her out, a smile on his rugged face now. A tremor of fear still moved through her.

Yes, she and Gage were supposed to spend the evening together. He'd even said he'd ordered dinner and dessert —and more pieces clicked into place. He *had* been planning to celebrate his birthday with her. He just hadn't told her yet.

"Hey, bud," Teddy said beside her. "We're on the island. Where are you?" He grinned from ear to ear. "I'm sure she's fine, buddy."

Sheryl wanted to talk to Gage, but she wanted to do it in private. She indicated to Teddy that she wanted to talk.

"In fact, she's right here. You want to say hello?"

Sheryl heard Gage yelling as Teddy extended the phone toward her, already laughing.

"...think you're so funny!" he finished just Sheryl put the phone to her ear. He audibly drew in a deep breath, and she began to see the comedy in the situation. "This is Sheryl, isn't it?"

"It's your birthday?" she asked, plenty of bite in her tone.

"You went along with this?" he barked back. "I called the cops, Sheryl. They're out looking for you."

"Rudy will call them," she said, turning to his fellow Marine. "He called the cops."

"Oh, boy," Rudy, tapped and swiped and lifted his phone to his ear. "He likes her more than I thought."

"Totally," Teddy said, pulling out a pair of shades and settling them on his face. "Better tell him we dognapped Britta too. He'll go postal."

"We're at my house," Sheryl said. "They have Britta, apparently. Might just want to bring yourself."

"Michael is picking up the food," Rudy said, leaning

away from his call. "Yes, hello." He focused back on his phone call, rattling off his Marine rank as if the emergency operator would know what it meant.

Sheryl didn't and she'd had Gage explain it to her once.

"And your brother—"

"I heard," he said.

"Are you mad?"

"Yes."

"They put me in the back of a van," Sheryl said, turning her back on his friends.

"I'm going to kill them," he said, his breathing quickening. "I'll be there in a few minutes." He hung up without saying anything else, and Sheryl handed the phone back to Teddy.

"I don't think he sees the humor." She started for the house. "But we can't stand out here. We'll melt." Exhaustion pulled through every muscle in her body, as it had been a long morning finishing the beach. Then she and Gage had shopped for the banana split party, and she'd hosted that and cleaned up afterward. She kind of wanted the slow, candlelit dinner Gage had promised her—but as Michael pulled up to the curb in front of her house and got out with a few huge bags of food, she knew she wasn't going to get it.

～

SHERYL WAS IN HER BEDROOM WHEN GAGE ARRIVED, AND she stayed there, needing him to have a moment to talk with his friends about what had happened. In the end, she was fine. So she'd ridden in the back of a van for five or six minutes—the total time from the inn to her beach cottage. She'd never been in any real danger.

She unlocked the door at the same time someone knocked on it, so she opened it almost immediately. Gage stood there, his features dark and stormy. Maybe his friends had done her a favor, because wow, he was sexy when he was angry.

"Are you okay?" he asked.

"Yes."

He visibly softened, but she wasn't done with him yet. "Is it really your birthday?"

"Yes." He ducked his head then.

"Why didn't you tell me?" She put her hand on his chest, feeling the warmth from his body against her palm. His pulse beat steadily, and she realized how attached to him she was. And she barely knew him.

In that moment, everything became crystal clear, and she fell back a step. "You should go celebrate with the people who love you." Sheryl hated how the words sounded, but she couldn't change them or pull them back in.

Gage blinked, surprise mixing with the fading fury. "Does that include you?"

"I don't know, Gage," she said. "You didn't even tell me it was your birthday."

"I was going to. Tonight. While we drifted in that hammock, and I fell more in love with you."

She heard what he said, but she didn't know what to do with it. "This feels fast," she said.

"It is fast." He looked down the hall and then back at her. "Please come eat. I got that barbecue you like, with all that coleslaw. Nobody else will eat the stuff. And if you want to break up with me tomorrow, fine. But it's my birthday, so you can't break up with me today."

Despite her mood, a smile sprang to her face. "Is that a rule?"

"Yes," he said simply. "You don't have a present for me, do you?"

Sadness hit her, and she shook her head. "I would've gotten you one, had I known."

"*You're* my gift," he said, reaching for her. Somehow, he'd managed to turn the moment sweet and romantic with just three words. "Please come eat with us."

She moved forward when he tugged, and he added, "I can introduce you to them properly."

"All right," she said. "But after everyone leaves, you have a *lot* of explaining to do."

"Deal," he said, pressing his lips to her forehead. Sheryl tried not to press into his touch. Tried, and failed, revealing that she'd started to fall for him too.

But that didn't mean she was happy with his choices.

14

"You've met Rudy and Teddy," Gage said, his stomach still swooping from left to right. He'd learned to control it in the military, but he'd been retired for a couple of years now. He knew how to handle stress, and he knew how to keep his eyes peeled for danger. He just hadn't had to deal with such things much here in Carter's Cove.

He glared at his friends, whose prank was certainly not funny.

"Yes," Sheryl said cordially. "I think Rudy was the one who pushed me into the van." She smiled as she said it, but Gage could hear the undercurrent of discomfort in her voice.

They laughed and Sheryl stepped into her own kitchen to start setting up the food. That was exactly what Gage didn't want her to do. She'd had a very long day, with several more to come. He did too. He just wanted a quiet night with his girlfriend, and his buddies had ruined it.

Thankfully, the police hadn't come over, and nothing had gone too far by the time Rudy called to let them know that Sheryl wasn't in any danger.

No, Gage was the one in trouble, and he knew it. Sheryl wasn't happy about the false kidnapping either, but that front was all because he hadn't told her about his birthday.

He moved into the kitchen to help her, mumbling under his breath. "I can do it, Sheryl."

"It's fine, Gage." She put distance between them as she got down cups and started making punch. Gage's relationship with her was new, but they'd spent an extraordinary amount of time together, and she hated entertaining.

For family functions, she'd told him that they went to her parents house or had events at the inn. That way, she didn't have to clean up. "Since I spend so much of my job cleaning up after people, I hate doing it at home too."

And she'd definitely have to clean up after four men, a dog, and herself. Gage turned when Michael said, "Let's have the cake first."

The candles were already stuck in the tall, round cake he'd obviously bought somewhere.

"That was your special order?" Sheryl asked, setting plates on the countertop. "My sister made that cake."

"It'll be great then," Gage said quickly, but Sheryl only

frowned at him before she rolled her eyes.

"Gage is a wizard in the kitchen," Teddy said. "Did you know that, Sheryl?"

"I've heard," she said. "He doesn't seem to have time to bake for me."

Gage froze, because the reason he didn't have time to bake for her was *because of her*. "Funny," he said dryly, turning to Rudy. "So what are you guys doing here?" He'd asked them a version of the same question while Sheryl hid in her bedroom. Neither of them had given him a good answer. Instead, they'd told him they'd come for his birthday.

"Celebrating with you," Rudy said.

"You said that already," he said, not caring if he made things awkward. They already were anyway. "But really. Why now?"

"Listen, man," Teddy said, clapping him on the shoulder. Gage looked at his hand and then looked at Teddy, and the other man removed his fingers from Gage's body. "The old windbag had surgery." He shrugged. "Thought you might like to go with us to visit him in the hospital."

Gage automatically rejected the idea. "I have two jobs I'm working right now," he said. Three, if he counted Sheryl, and managing his relationship with her was definitely a full-time job, one he had no idea how to do.

"We can go whenever," Rudy said. "Doesn't have to be when he's in the hospital. He had a hip replaced. He's got a long recovery ahead of him."

"Who's the old windbag?" Sheryl asked. "For those of us not in the Marines."

"I like her," Teddy said, beaming at Sheryl. She smiled back at him, the gesture fading when she moved her gaze to Gage.

"Our sergeant," Gage said.

"I thought you were a sergeant," Sheryl said, her beautiful eyes coloring with confusion.

"He is," Teddy said. "I was Staff Sergeant, one step above him. The old windbag is our Master Sergeant. Led our whole group."

"Makes sense," Sheryl said, but Gage knew in her mind, it didn't.

"He was my boss," Gage said. "Sort of like Olympia is your boss."

"My sister is not my boss," she snapped, deflating in the next moment. "I'm sorry. I'm just tired. Let's sing."

Gage couldn't look anywhere but at her. Everyone else watched him. "You heard her," he said, his voice dangerously quiet. "Let's sing. Michael?"

"Do you have any matches?" he asked Sheryl. "A lighter?"

"Oh, sure." She opened a drawer and produced what he wanted. She was organized, right down to the inventory in her kitchen, and Gage sure did like that. Michael lit the candles—thankfully, there were not forty of them—and by the glow of the fire, the men started to sing.

Sheryl joined her higher voice with theirs, but it was

clear she was used to a more sophisticated type of birthday party. Not the laughing, ribbing, pushing kind Rudy and Teddy were doing.

Still, by the end of the song, Gage was smiling with his friends. "Thank you," he said, admitting to himself that maybe celebrating his birthday with friends was better than what he'd planned.

"Blow 'em out, Sergeant," Rudy said. "Make your wish."

"I know what he's wishing," Teddy said.

"Yeah, for you to can it." Gage glared, took a big breath, and blew out the candles. Michael and Sheryl clapped, and then his brother said, "Okay, food. Let's eat."

Gage loaded up his plate and took it into the living room, Britta right at his heels. He fed her a piece of chicken from his plate and eyed Sheryl until she sat in the recliner on his right. Teddy sat next to him, and Gage asked, "Are you thinking of retiring?"

"I mean, maybe," he said. "I don't have a pretty island or a pretty woman to come home to." He took a bite of his fried chicken, a moan following it. "Wow, this is fantastic."

"It comes from a local place here on the island," Gage said. "Sheryl told me about it, and I've been wanting to try it." He looked at her, glad she was eating and not glaring his face off. He did have some explaining to do, but he hoped he could punctuate his sentences with kisses, so she wouldn't be quite so angry.

He'd felt her lean into his touch down the hall several

minutes ago. She liked him. He just didn't know how to have a girlfriend, and he hoped it wouldn't cost him the one he currently had.

BY THE TIME GAGE GOT HIS MARINE BUDDIES AND HIS brother out of Sheryl's house, darkness was falling. He closed the door behind Michael and pressed his back into the wood. A long hiss came out of his mouth, and he tracked Sheryl as she moved in her kitchen on the other side of the cottage.

"I'm so sorry," he said. "I didn't know they would do something like this."

"Obviously," she said.

"I didn't even know Rudy was back in the country." And he'd looked good. Rudy had been through a lot, and he deserved to be happy. "Let's leave all this and go lay in the hammock." He put his hand over hers, stopping her from picking up another plate. "Come on. I'll clean it up later."

"It's already later," she said, not meeting his eye.

"Sheryl." Gage drew her into his arms, glad she succumbed and wrapped her arms around him.

"Okay," she said. "I have been wanting to lay in the hammock."

"With me?"

"With you." She glanced up at him. "But I want you to talk for the first fifteen minutes."

"Fifteen minutes straight?" Horror darted through Gage.

She giggled, the sound morphing into a full-blown laugh. Relief spread through Gage, and he led her out the back door to the tree at the corner of the house. He'd hung the hammock there, and he collapsed into it first, then cradled her against his chest. They fit perfectly together, and he sighed a long, happy sigh.

"I'm sorry I didn't tell you about my birthday. I just wanted a quiet, romantic night with the two of us."

"Mm."

"When I didn't see you in that office...I can't even describe what I was thinking."

"It was a scary ten minutes."

"They must've taken you right before I got there," he said. "What happened? Why did you go with them?"

"Why did I go with them?" she repeated, her voice pitching up. "Have you met your Marine friends, Gage? One of their arms weighs more than I do. I didn't have a choice."

"You left your phone."

"Okay." She pushed herself up. "This is the opposite of relaxing. I changed my mind. I don't want to listen to tell me how wrong I was, and what I should've done different for the next fifteen minutes."

She managed to get out of the hammock, even if she did make him swing wildly.

"I'm sorry," he called after her, the last of the light of the day fading right before his eyes. The stars started to wink in the sky above him, and he just wanted Sheryl to come back.

She didn't.

Gage waited as long as he could, and then he got up and followed her inside. She'd left the kitchen for him to clean, and he set about doing that. "Happy birthday to me," he muttered.

"I would've told you happy birthday the moment I woke up," she said, her voice angry and coming from behind him. "*You* robbed me of that opportunity."

He turned toward her. "I didn't want to make it a big deal. I knew you were busy."

"You don't get to decide what I do or don't do," she said. "I'm a grown woman, and I can manage my time the way I see fit." Her fingers curled into fists. "I like you Gage. I want to get to know more about you, and kiss you in the hammock, and celebrate holidays and birthdays with you. But I can't do that with someone who keeps pushing me away."

"I'm not pushing you away."

"You are," she said. "Or you're at least keeping the door part-way closed, your whole body weight behind it." She sighed, the exhaustion entering her face again. "I don't want to fight with you. If you don't want to be with me, just say it."

"I don't want that at all," he said. "I want to spend all my free time with you. All of it." He watched Britta go over to Sheryl and sit on her feet, leaning her weight into the human. "I'm just really bad at this."

"Define this."

"Having a girlfriend. I'm good at following directions. Reading tactical plans. Watching people on the ferry and on a beach. But I'm not super great at this." He gestured between the two of them. "I'm doing the best I can. Maybe it's not good enough for you."

His chest heaved as he breathed again. He didn't want to leave things like this with her. He'd never felt too terribly inferior to her, but she definitely had more money than he did. She stuck to the ritziest parts of the island while he ate footlongs on the benches down in South Port. She ran a grounds crew of over sixty people, and she and her sister ran the entire Heartwood Inn empire.

She was way out of his league, and maybe he should end things right now.

But his heart didn't want to. And for once, his brain and his heart were on the same page.

"It's good enough for me," she said, and Gage crossed the room to her and cradled her face in his hands.

Tonight had not been exactly what he wanted. Not even close to what he wanted. But he did lean down and get his birthday kiss.

15

*S*heryl survived the surfing competition by the skin of her teeth. She didn't see Gage much, and she actually thought they benefitted from the cooling off period. She was able to move past his omission about his birthday, and she was sitting in her office a day or two after the beaches had cleared when she got a text from Celeste.

O needs us. Her penthouse. Stat.

On my way, Gwen answered at the same time Sheryl was typing.

Coming up, she said.

Be there in a sec, Alissa said. Sheryl was already out the door, because if her sister needed her, she'd be there. That was one of the blessings of the five of them working the inn. They each had a vital role, but they could be there for one another.

She met Gwen in the lobby, and she pushed the elevator button. "What do you think the problem is?" Gwen asked.

"Her boyfriend," Sheryl said. "Olympia needs to get out of her own way."

"Still hung up on Hunter?"

"She's not hung up on him," Sheryl said. "She was broken by him, and I don't think she's pieced herself back together quite yet." The elevator dinged, but the door was so slow to open. "It's a shame, because her boyfriend is hot."

The doors opened and the man Sheryl had met at the bonfire stood there. Chet himself looked up, and Sheryl could only stare at him. "Ladies," he said, and Gwen actually twittered as he stepped off the elevator.

Sheryl got on, grabbing Gwen's hand and towing her onto the car too. "That's him."

"Who?" Gwen asked, a sense of wonder still in her voice.

"Olympia's boyfriend. Was he carrying a bag?" She tried to look, but the doors slid closed, and the ride up to the penthouse began. When she and Gwen got to Olympia's apartment, they found Celeste cleaning up ice cream containers and Olympia lying on the couch, nothing curled or pressed or straight, the way it usually was.

"Oh, it's bad," Gwen said, looking at Sheryl.

It was bad, and Sheryl didn't know what to do about it.

She wondered if this could be her in a week, or two weeks, or a month, or two months. Had she given her heart to Gage to squeeze the life from it whenever he felt like it?

She participated in the conversation, but she couldn't help wondering if she was destined for the same fate as her older sister.

When she left Olympia's suite, she found Gage leaning against the wall, looking at his phone. He glanced up when the door opened, and a smile brightened his face. He was devilishly good-looking, and Sheryl's heart pumped out several extra beats. She wasn't sure if she was excited to see him there or annoyed.

"What are you doing here?" she asked.

"Waiting for you."

She looked at her phone. "I didn't get a text."

"That's because I didn't text." He embraced her, his lips skating down her neck. "Aren't you proud of me?"

"I sure am," Celeste said, entering the hall too.

Sheryl jumped away from Gage, though she liked where he'd been going.

Celeste definitely had everything pressed and in its proper place, her light blonde hair falling in curls over her shoulders. She looked at Sheryl with a sparkle in her eye and added, "Aren't you going to introduce me to your boyfriend?"

"Yes," Sheryl said at the same time Gage said, "I'm Gage Sanders," and extended his hand toward Celeste.

"Celeste," she said.

"Second-oldest," he said, glancing at Sheryl, who stood there like an accessory. "Right?"

"Right," Celeste and Sheryl said at the same time. She hated being an extra in the conversation, and Gage hadn't even given her a chance to introduce Celeste. Of course, neither had her sister. But Celeste had always been a little overbearing. She wanted just as much control as Olympia, but she wasn't the oldest Heartwood sister, so she'd fought constantly for a power position.

"He's my bodyguard," Sheryl said, drawing both Celeste's and Gage's eyes to her. "I mean, that's how we started."

"Well, I'm late for a meeting," Celeste said, smiling at Sheryl and Gage before walking to the incredibly slow elevator.

Gage watched her go, and Sheryl couldn't seem to look away until her sister got on the elevator and left too.

"I'm your bodyguard?" he asked, and Sheryl knew she'd made a mistake.

"I mean, that *is* how we met."

Gage exhaled and looked away. "Are you still working, or can we go to lunch?"

Sheryl's insides felt encased in gelatin, and they wobbled. "I still have work to do."

Something moved between them, and Gage nodded. "All right. Do you...?"

"You look like you could use a nap," Sheryl said. "I'm

fine. I don't need you to take me home in the afternoons anymore."

Gage just stared at her, his jaw clenched and those midnight eyes drinking her up. "All right," he said, turning and heading for the elevator.

She wasn't sure what had just happened, but she knew she couldn't stand there in the hall while the infuriatingly slow elevator came back up from the lobby. "See you later," she said, ducking back into Olympia's penthouse, where Alissa and Gwen still sat with their sister.

She pressed her back into the door and breathed.

"Are you okay?" Gwen asked.

"Fine," Sheryl said, straightening. "I just...needed to use the bathroom. Is that okay, O?"

"Go right ahead," Olympia said. She looked better after a sisterly intervention, but Sheryl felt on the verge of a break-down, and she didn't even know why.

Locked in the bathroom, she looked at herself in the mirror, trying to find the reason she'd told Celeste Gage was her bodyguard. He'd been so much more than that from the moment they'd met.

Her phone chimed, and she hastily pulled it from her pocket. *Are you trying to put distance between us?* Gage had asked.

Sheryl honestly didn't know.

I'm going to South Port for lunch. Call me if you need me.

Sheryl put her phone on the vanity and looked into her eyes again. When she'd first met Gage, she did need him. Needed him to get her home without incident. Needed him to stay with her, so Ricky wouldn't cause a problem. Needed him to feel safe.

But now?

Did she *need* him?

She hated that she didn't know the answer. And she hated his next text too. *Thanks for the work. If you know anyone else looking for a bodyguard, let me know.*

LATER THAT DAY, SHERYL LAY IN THE HAMMOCK, WATCHING the leaves above her move with the wind. She wasn't sure what had happened that afternoon, but she knew such situations would probably keep occurring. One thought had been revolving in her mind: *Maybe Gage just isn't the one for you.*

And maybe he wasn't.

She didn't call him that day, nor the next. He didn't show up at the inn in the afternoons, and the silence between them felt thick and dense. Sheryl didn't know how to break it, so she just let it go on and on.

That weekend, the farmer's market found her wandering through the aisles, a recyclable shopping bag over her arm as she picked out the fruits and vegetables she wanted. The crowd had good energy, and she loved the vibrancy of colors in each booth, the clean, crisp scent of the air, the pure sunshine overhead.

She loved summertime in Carter's Cove, and she couldn't wait to get home and make a smoothie with all of her new fruits. She thought of Gage, and where he might be. Probably not the farmer's market in downtown. Probably in South Port, where all the hipsters and artsy types hung out.

Funny, she didn't consider him a hipster or artsy. Sure, he liked to bake, but he didn't paint or weave or make jewelry. He rode a sleek, black motorcycle, for crying out loud. Sheryl did miss riding on the back of that motorcycle, but she couldn't use that as one of the reasons she wanted to keep Gage in her life.

It had been four days since they'd last talked, in person or via text, and Sheryl realized in that moment that she hated not being able to talk to him. She wished he were there with her, at the farmer's market, picking out apples for a tart he'd make for her later that day.

She pulled out her phone and called him, her pulse bobbing somewhere in the back of her throat.

"Hey, I'm on a job," he said by way of hello.

"Oh, okay," she said. "I didn't know you worked the ferry on weekends."

"I don't. It's a private gig."

"Oh. I just—I'm at the farmer's market, and I wondered if you wanted to join me. But I guess you can't."

"I can't."

"I'll call you later?"

"Okay." And with that, the call ended. Sheryl actually

looked at her phone to make sure he hadn't just gone silent. He hadn't barked, but his brusque, abrupt nature had returned in full force.

He was on a job, she told herself as she turned to cross over to a new row of stalls. She'd come to the market alone, and she'd pushed him away. Now she just had to figure out how to bring him back in.

Maybe we could see each other tonight? She typed out the words and sent them to him, hoping whatever job he was working would allow texting. He'd taken a call from her, so she was hopeful.

Sure, his text came back, and everything inside Sheryl relaxed. Couples went through ups and downs, and maybe she'd just needed a minute to collect her breath. Find her center. Realize she did like Gage and want to continue getting to know him.

Fine, she really liked Gage, and she wanted to get on the same page with him, and then kiss him that evening.

Satisfied with her plans, she continued down the booths, buying what she thought looked good. Her phone rang, and she swiped on the call from Javier. "Is Melinda having that baby?"

"Yes," he said. "She is. We just got to the hospital, and I can't remember if I even closed the front door. Will you go by and check?"

"Of course," Sheryl said. "Did you take everything you needed?"

"I honestly have no idea."

Sheryl laughed, excited about the new baby too. "Javier, go be with Melinda. Call me if you need anything. I'm not working this weekend." She had a skeletal crew at the inn, because everyone needed time off after the huge surfing competition. They'd all hit it hard next week as July started to become August and more debris came from the trees on the property.

"Okay," Javier said. "I just wanted to let you know."

"Thanks." Sheryl hung up, still smiling. She sighed as she slipped her phone in her purse. A familiar voice reached her ears, and surprise lifted her eyebrows as she started searching for Gage.

He was here?

She found him easily, a few booths down from her, his arm linked through another blonde woman's.

Horror and disbelief froze her to the spot. What was he doing? He called cheating on her a *job*?

The couple looked up, and Sheryl recognized the women. Lisa Talley, another Carter's Cove local.

Gage's eyes met hers, and he froze too.

Sheryl spun away from him, everything from her past crashing through her memory.

"Sheryl," he called, but she didn't wait, turn, or go back. She couldn't face him right now, and she needed to get out of the crowd before she started crying.

16

"Hey, I need a minute," Gage said, tracking Sheryl as she moved through the crowd. Dang, the woman could move fast when she wanted to.

Lisa looked up at him. "All right. Who's Sheryl?'

"My real girlfriend," he said, slipping his arm out hers. "Can I have a minute? You'll be okay?"

"Oh, my heck, yes. Go."

And Gage went, jogging through the crowd, easily keeping Sheryl's ponytail in sight. "Sheryl," he said again when he got close to her, and this time, she turned back to him. "Wait a second."

"Are you seeing Lisa Talley?"

"She's my new client," he said, his chest heaving though he hadn't been running particularly fast or for very long. "Her old boyfriend is giving her trouble. She asked me to pretend to be her new boyfriend."

"How convenient."

"It's not what you think." He looked at her, so many emotions storming inside his chest. She was so beautiful, and so upset. "I'm not cheating on you." How could he tell her that he'd fallen in love with her now? She'd cut him out of her life for the past four days, and a river of hurt flowed through him.

She swiped at her eyes and lifted her chin. "You're not?"

"Of course not." He shook his head. "I can't believe you'd think I would."

"Yeah, well, you thought I'd let Rudy and Teddy take me from my office."

Anger joined his hurt feelings. "I didn't mean that."

"You're just 'doing the best you can,' right?"

"Yes," he said, barking the word. "And you're the one who couldn't even introduce me as your boyfriend to your sister."

"I did," she said, though Gage's recollection of those awkward moments in the hall was that Sheryl had just stood there—at least until she felt the need to remind him of what he was to her.

Subservient.

Her bodyguard.

He'd been wrestling with his feelings of inadequacy alone for days, and they all reared up and started shouting at him.

"If I'm not good enough for you, you should just say it," he said, not bothering to make his voice quiet or kind.

"I've never said that."

"No, you just act like it every time we're together in front of someone you care about. You're worried about me making you look bad."

Sheryl shook her head. "I thought we were past that."

"We were, until you couldn't tell Celeste who I was. And you won't go to South Port with me. Instead, you're up here at this hoity toity farmer's market. We never go to my place; always yours." He shook his head, because all of these poisonous thoughts had been festering inside for days. He hated them and wanted them gone, but saying them out loud to Sheryl wouldn't fix anything.

In fact, he felt like he was breaking their relationship.

"Look, Lisa's paying me for two weeks of a fake relationship," he said. "It's good money, and I took the job."

"Good for you," she said.

"You're lucky you don't need two jobs, Sheryl," he said, wishing she'd at least try to see how everyone else lived, recognize the problems they dealt with. "Some of us aren't Heartwoods, you know."

Pure fury crossed her face. "Go back to your other girlfriend. And I don't need you to come over tonight."

"Are we breaking up?" he asked. It would almost be a relief. Maybe then, he could stop thinking about her. Wondering if he should call or stop by the inn. Losing sleep.

"Yes," she said. "We're breaking up." She turned and strode away, her designer purse swaying violently on her arm.

Gage watched her go, part of his heart withering to dust. Several moments later, Lisa joined him. "Looks like it didn't go well."

"No," he said. "It didn't."

BY THAT EVENING, GAGE REALIZED THAT NOT JUST PART OF his heart had turned to dust, but the whole thing. He slumped on the couch, staring at the TV while Michael talked about something. He honestly wasn't listening, because if he did, he'd only be annoyed on top of angry and broken-hearted. He just wanted to be alone. Have his kitchen and his bathroom to himself again. His afternoons to bake something, make a mess, throw a ball to Britta.

Ever since he'd gotten that text from Tyler, everything in his life had changed. He'd changed.

"Gage?"

He finally turned and looked at his brother. "Hmm?"

"Did you hear what I said? I'll be out of your hair soon."

He straightened, part of him not wanting his brother to go, when literally ten seconds ago, that was all he wanted. "You will? Why? Did you talk to Marie?"

"I did, and we're going to try to make things work." Michael smiled at him. "So I'll get packed up tonight and tomorrow. Take the ferry back in the evening."

"That's great," he said, and he meant it. "I'm glad, Michael. You and Marie have always been so good together."

"Like you and Sheryl."

Gage gave a short, barking laugh. "She broke up with me."

"What?" Michael looked truly shocked. "When?"

"Tuesday," he said though today was Saturday. "I don't know. We're from two different worlds." He didn't want to look around his tiny beach house and compare it to hers. He paid for his. Hers belonged to her family. He shouldn't be bitter that she had more than him. The Heartwoods had obviously worked for a lot of years to have what they had. He didn't begrudge anyone for having things, especially when they'd worked hard.

And Sheryl worked hard, so he wasn't sure why he was so annoyed with her.

"I'm sorry," Michael said, turning off the TV. "Maybe it'll be like me and Marie. Maybe she just needs some time to think through things."

"Maybe." Gage watched Michael stand up and head for the bedrooms.

"I'm going to go pack."

"Okay." Gage leaned back into the couch again, his

mind constantly rotating around Sheryl. He didn't think she needed time to think through anything. What she needed time to do was overcome her embarrassment of him.

She'd never had a problem with him when he was just her bodyguard. Or when they kissed in the privacy of her office. Or hung out at her house. Other than those times, the only time she was comfortable around him was with her mother and grandmother. He still hadn't met her father yet, and that was probably a good thing.

He sighed, and Britta perked up. "Yeah?" he asked, though he wasn't sure what the dog was trying to say. "Should we take a walk down the beach?"

Britta got up, an earnest look on her face, and took a few steps toward the back door. That was definitely her doggy version of *Yes, please. Walk.*

Gage got up too and followed her. He left her leash in the house, because she wouldn't go too far from him. Very few people used this beach in the evenings. Only locals, and while his house did sit two hundred yards from the waves, it wasn't a ritzy or a well-kept beach.

"Let's go then. Mike, I'm going for a walk."

"Okay," his brother called from inside the house. Gage left, pulling the door closed behind him and making sure he had his phone. He did, and he went down the steps, feeling an ache in his muscles he wished would go away.

He probably shouldn't have taken that job with Lisa Talley. The money was good, but he could've dipped into his pension, which he'd been saving. But he'd been so upset with Sheryl. Regret filled him as the sky continued to darken by degrees.

"I need to take some time off," he said to himself, only the wind for a companion. Britta had taken off down the beach, chasing a gull. He whistled to her, and she came running back, a huge grin on her face.

"Stay by me," he said, squishing his way through the softer sand toward the wetter, more packed stuff closer to the water's edge. Once he reached it, he turned north and started walking. If he went all the way around the horn of the island and back down the east side, he'd run into Sheryl's place. He'd mapped it once, and it was just over three miles, and certainly not something he'd do on a nightly stroll.

He breathed in the night air, wishing the rising moon would give him some advice. The thought that he didn't need to work as much came to him again, and he swiped on his phone. After navigating to his bank app, he pulled up his accounts and paused.

"Brit, wait," he said, and the dog slowed and trotted back to him. He scanned the numbers in his two accounts, one savings and one checking. He wasn't an extravagant man, and he could get by with just the ferry job.

Looking up, the night seemed so much darker as his adjusted away from the phone screen. "Okay, girl," he told the dog. "No more extra jobs. Just the ferry in the morning. You'll have to stop pigging out on my leftovers."

And he might have to cut back on his baking. He hadn't been doing that since he'd started dating Sheryl, and his grocery budget had been much smaller.

Problem was, if he didn't have another job in the afternoon, and no girlfriend, baking was all he had left to fill his time.

"So you'll find another hobby," he said. "A free one. Walking on the beach. Painting at South Port."

Something. He'd figure out something, because he didn't particularly enjoy being someone's fake boyfriend, even if the money was good.

Except for Sheryl. He'd be her fake anything, for free.

He sighed again and started walking. Britta went with him, her nose touching his hand as if she understood what he was feeling. He wasn't sure she did, because he could barely identify the emotions streaming through him.

"I know," he said. "I miss her so much."

The last few days had been brutal, and Gage had texted everyone he'd ever done a job for, even a small one. He'd drummed up Lisa pretty quickly after that, and he'd only had to spend one afternoon with himself.

There was a marked difference between Lisa and Sheryl, and there had been from the get-go. Sheryl made his blood run hot and his heart pound in a way no other woman had. Lisa was pretty, but she wasn't his type.

"Sheryl's not either," he muttered, but it simply wasn't

true. Just because she was soft where he was hard didn't make them incompatible.

Maybe Michael was right. Maybe Gage just needed to give her some time to cool off, and then he could try to win her back.

17

*S*heryl weeded with a vengeance, determined to clear the overlooked bed that hadn't been tended to in weeks. The inn's three swimming pools sat down the sidewalk a ways, and this area of the grounds wasn't used by guests. But it should still look pristine, and Sheryl wiped the sweat off her forehead and reached a gloved hand for another weed.

Javier hadn't been to work in days as he dealt with becoming a new father. Sheryl had gone to visit him and Melinda and their new baby boy in the hospital, and she was going again that night.

She had to have something scheduled in the evenings so she wouldn't go crazy. Or go find Gage and beg him to come back to her. Which was also crazy. She'd sat down with a pen and a paper—no computer. No phone—and she'd made a list of all the reasons they weren't right for each other.

She read it every day when she got to work, just to remind herself that she could make it through the hours that came after two p.m. without him.

She'd done it for four days now, and each one had been excruciating. The time moved so slowly, and the activities around the island didn't hold the same magic without him at her side. So she'd stayed home, but being caged by walls had been terrible.

After eating one dinner with her parents and grandmother, she'd decided she couldn't stomach doing that more than once or twice a week. Three times, if she was desperate. She loved her parents, but her mother asked a lot of questions, and her father kept inviting her to go fishing. And without Gage occupying her time, Sheryl had actually considered going.

That was when she'd realized she'd hit rock bottom.

Last night, she'd invited Tyler and Abby over for dinner, and it had been the first time she didn't feel like suffocating inside her own house.

So tonight, she'd take Melinda dinner and spend time with her friends. She wouldn't be alone, and everything would be fine.

Except Sheryl knew it wouldn't be. Somehow, in the short time she'd known Gage Sanders, he'd embedded himself in her heart. Sheryl had considerable access to the gossip circles around the island, and while she never wanted to be featured on them, she'd been able to find out about Lisa Talley and her ex-boyfriend with two texts and ten minutes of her time.

She hired someone to be her boyfriend, Victoria had texted. Between you and me, of course. It's a secret, so Rob won't know. Shh.

Sheryl wasn't going to tell anyone. In fact, she hated herself a little bit for even texting the former homecoming queen that had never left the island and still acted like they were in high school. But Victoria Gibson knew all the gossip, and she'd given it to Sheryl easily.

How her relationship with Gage had stayed off Victoria's radar, she wasn't sure. Probably because Sheryl worked seven days a week, and Gage was an unknown on the island.

He'd always accused her of thinking him beneath her, and the moment she thought it, her blood turned hot. She didn't care if they went to her beach cottage or his. She never had.

No, she hadn't been to South Port, and the idea to spend one of her now-free afternoons down there entered her mind again. It wasn't the first time the thought had come to her, and she was starting to think someone was prompting her.

She groaned as she stretched her back and looked up into the sky. "Is that what You want me to do?" she asked, as if she had a relationship with God and He'd tell her.

"Fine," she said when she felt nothing, and no one answered. "I'll go to South Port."

A FEW MORE DAYS PASSED BEFORE SHERYL ACTUALLY WENT through with her promise to herself. But Sunday afternoon found her tipping the pedicab driver and turning toward the beach in South Port. Somewhere along the boardwalk, a band played, and she started walking toward the sound.

This area of the island did have a unique feel. It was older, and it used to be the vibrant, lively part of the island, before one of the major hurricanes had wiped it out. Main Street had been moved inland a bit, and father east, toward the inn.

Her family had benefitted from that move greatly, and she didn't have to be ashamed of that. She wasn't. But she could acknowledge it.

The boardwalk along the beach here led right down to the sand, where groups of people had gathered to enjoy the sun and the surf. One group listened to a teenage boy plucking on his guitar, and Sheryl found herself smiling in that direction. She would've loved to have come to South Port when she was a teen. Her father wouldn't have approved, and as one of the younger sisters, such an act— even in the middle of a Sunday afternoon like today— would've gotten her some attention.

As it was, Sheryl had learned to follow and obey rules. She loved gardening, and it just worked out that the inn needed someone with her green thumbs to run the landscaping and grounds crew.

"One dollar sliders," a man said, handing her a flyer. "Down the boardwalk at the food truck."

Sheryl wondered if this was the same truck where Gage got his beloved hot dogs. Her stubborn streak reared its ugly head, and she squashed it down. She'd come to South Port to enjoy herself, not obsess about Gage.

But this place screamed his name, and she could imagine an evening here with him. It would be romantic and wonderful, and Sheryl's chest pinched. She felt like she hadn't drawn a full, proper breath since the farmer's market just over a week ago, and the only person who could help her get the oxygen she needed was Gage.

She continued down the boardwalk toward the band and found half a dozen food trucks set up in a semi-circle. The beach spread before them, and easily twice as many people dotted this beach as the one she'd left behind.

The long storm wall filled with murals stretched down the other way, past the food trucks, and Sheryl determined she'd get something to eat and then admire the art on the beach. Food. Art. Beach. No wonder Gage loved this place.

She spotted the truck where she could get the foot-long, and she joined the line there. She'd only eaten from food trucks like this a couple of other times, and she hoped she wouldn't embarrass herself too badly.

After managing to order and pay, she got her hot dog and walked down into the sand. It was hot and covered her sandaled feet. The wall ran before her on the left, and it was filled with vibrant colors and pieces of art that over-lapped each other in various messages of hope and love.

She saw things like Soda Snake and Burgers and Birds, two places she'd loved as a little girl. She hadn't thought about them in a long time, and a sense of nostalgia hit her when she hadn't been expecting it.

All the benches were full, so she found a spot on the boardwalk and sat down to eat her footlong. She smiled as she squeezed ketchup and mustard out of little packets to go with the sautéed onions she'd requested.

"Here we go," she said, wishing with everything in her that Gage was there with her. It felt like a moment that would bond them forever, and Sheryl paused.

"I'm in love with him," she whispered, feeling it and knowing what she'd just admitted to herself was true.

Then she took a bite of her footlong, the heat of the dog almost burning her mouth. "Oh, my heck," she said, her mouth still full. That was the most delicious thing she'd eaten in a long time. As she ate the twelve inches of meaty goodness, all she could think about was how she could get Gage back into her life.

She knew he liked to bake, and she wondered if she could show up at his beach house with a perfect apple tart, an apology, and a plea for him to forgive her. But her skills with pastry probably wouldn't pass kindergarten, and she thought she should probably just take him a foot-long and call it good.

The more that idea existed in her mind, the better it sounded. But she'd want the food to be hot and delicious, and she had no idea if Gage would even be home right now. A Sunday afternoon date was probably high on Lisa's list of things to do to convince her ex she'd moved on. Sheryl didn't want to be left sitting on Gage's steps, waiting for him to come home from a date with another woman.

Even if it wasn't a real date.

So she wadded up her tin foil wrapper, got up, and threw her trash away. After a quick stop at the grocery store, she rummaged through her cupboards until she found an apron. An Internet search brought up an apple tart recipe, and Sheryl washed her hands with a great deal of hope in her heart.

Two hours later, she admitted defeat when the second tart came out of the oven looking like charred soup. How such a thing was possible, she didn't know. But flour dusted every surface in the kitchen, her sink held a ton of apple skins and cores, and she hadn't been able to get the first tart out of the pan. So she'd thrown it away.

"That one was too dense," she said, wiping her hair off her sweaty face. "This one is runny. I don't get it." She'd used the same recipe both times and gotten wildly different results.

So baking wasn't going to cut it. She heaved a sigh and dumped the sloppy tart into the trashcan. At least her house smelled like pie crust and cinnamon, even if she didn't have anything edible to show for it.

She wouldn't be getting Gage back through her baking. What could she do instead?

18

*G*age rolled up to The Heartwood Inn as he'd done countless times before. This time, though, trepidation had his heart skipping in his chest the way small children did. He wasn't there to see Sheryl, but he could very easily run into her while on the premises. If he'd have called her before this interview, he probably wouldn't have to even go through with it.

He'd never met Alissa face-to-face, though he had spoken to her on the phone about the full-time position in the bakery. He already got up before dawn to work on the ferry, and he figured he'd rather get up and bake than get up and stroll around a boat, looking angry all the time.

He stowed his helmet and tugged at the bottom of his shirt. He wore slacks and a button-up; the same type of thing he'd worn to that upscale bonfire weeks ago. Inside the lobby, he saw a small sign that said *Bakery interviews:*

floor 3, and he stepped over to the elevator with relief. Sheryl would have no reason to be on the third floor. Still, he couldn't help thinking of her down on the lower level, probably in her office if she wasn't out on the grounds somewhere.

On the third floor, he followed the signs to a suite in the corner and checked in with a woman sitting at a desk there. She sported dark hair, so he knew she wasn't a Heartwood sister. He sat on the couch, early for his interview and glad of it, because it had taken a few minutes to get to the right place.

"Thanks for coming," a woman said, causing him to glance up. For one terrible moment, he thought he'd heard Sheryl. But it had been another blonde, this one definitely related to the woman he couldn't stop thinking about.

"You must be Gage," she said, approaching him. "I'm Alissa Heartwood."

"Gage Sanders." He stood and shook her hand, watching her for any sign of recognition. He saw none, and another wave of relief hit him.

She started for the door that led into the bedroom. "Nice to finally meet you, Gage."

"Finally?" he asked, following her. An alarm went off in his mind, but he couldn't figure out where to place it.

"We'll be starting with a taste test," Alissa said, ducking into the room.

Gage strode after her, because she'd practically run

away from him. He went through the doorway and paused, assessing everything he could see before he committed to staying in this room.

There was no bed in the room. Just a big table with several desserts on it. If they could even be classified as desserts. They looked like science experiments gone bad, and he frowned. Looking around the room, he couldn't see anyone else.

"Alissa?" Two other doors led out of this room, besides the closet, and another alarm went off. He took a step backward, thinking these Heartwoods might be a brand of crazy he didn't want to deal with.

"Hello, Gage."

He stilled, because that *was* Sheryl's voice. His attention jerked to his left, and sure enough, she stood there with her hair pulled up tight into that top ponytail, a pair of dangling earrings in her ears, and a fun, flirty sundress in pink and yellow.

The breath left his body, and he couldn't form words. Behind him, the clunk of the hotel room door closing registered in his mind, but it was still running pretty slow.

"You look great," she said, taking a couple of steps toward him.

"Thanks." He cleared the roughness from his voice. "So do you. What are you doing here?"

"I was going to ask you that." She smiled as she reached him. Only a couple of feet separated them, and he could easily take her into his arms and kiss her. Oh, how he wanted to do exactly that. Instead, he held very still.

"I'm applying to be the head baker here," he said. "Similar hours to the ferry."

"So you'd give up the ferry job?" she asked.

"Yes."

"And are you still Lisa's pretend boyfriend?"

"No."

"Are you looking to be someone's boyfriend?"

Gage shook his head. "Not particularly."

"Oh." She side-stepped over to the table. "Alissa said I could do this interview." She looked down at the dessert disasters. "You have to sample these and tell me what you think it is."

Gage walked over to the table, his stomach yelling at his mouth not to taste anything on this table. "This is...an interesting interview."

She handed him a fork, a sexy smile on her face that Gage wanted to kiss away. He took the fork and moved up and down the table, trying to find the tiniest piece of something that didn't look raw or overbaked.

"Who made these?" he asked. If it was the current head baker, no wonder the inn needed a new one.

"That's not important," Sheryl said.

Gage cocked one eyebrow at her and dug his fork into what he thought was a peach pie. He'd been born and raised in Georgia and knew what one should taste and look like. This had the right smell to it, even if it looked like it had been mixed with cream and then baked.

"Peach pie," he said, putting the tiny bite into his mouth. "Oh, yeah. It even tastes like it. There's just some… charred notes I'm not used to." He coughed slightly and put the fork down. This job wasn't worth eating these desserts.

He turned back to Sheryl. "It's so good to see you," he said, deciding to just say whatever came to his mind.

"I made the desserts," she said. "They're all my horrible, failed attempts at baking." She stepped closer to him. "See, I've been trying to get one decent thing made, so I could bring it to you and apologize."

She touched his chest, the heat from her hand like a brand. Her fingers moved up to his collar, and Gage fought against the raging river of desire moving through him.

"I'm sorry, Gage. I've been terrible to you." She looked up at him. "I went to South Port last weekend. That footlong is delicious, and the band playing was pretty fantastic."

"You went to South Port?"

"My next idea was to bring you a footlong and beg you to take me back," she whispered. "But every time I went by your house, your bike wasn't there." She looked like she was one breath away from crying, and her cheeks held a beautiful blush Gage wanted to see every day of his life.

"You want me to take you back?" He really needed to

stop asking questions, but some of the things she'd said didn't seem to make sense the first time.

"I'm in love with you," she said, and Gage blinked.

"Really?"

"Yes, really." She laughed lightly. "Is that so hard to believe?"

"A little, actually," he said.

Sheryl nodded, but she didn't look away from him. "We're not so different, you and I," she said. "We just need to learn how to communicate."

He agreed with that assessment, and his hand came up to rest on her hip. She didn't move away or flinch, and Gage finally caught up to what was happening here. "I'm not going to get the job, am I?" he asked, ducking his head so his mouth was closer to her ear.

"Oh, you'll get it if you want it," she said.

"Yeah?"

"Yes," she said, leaning away from him slightly so she could look at him. "The real question is whether you can forgive me. And whether you want *me* or not."

"Neither of those are real questions," Gage said. "Of course I want you." He closed his eyes and leaned his forehead against hers. "I've always wanted you, Sheryl. From the moment I laid eyes on you, I wanted you."

"Mm."

"And I can forgive you. Heaven knows I'm not perfect."

"You don't have to be."

He opened his eyes, and he saw the truth right there in

hers. She was right, and she believed what she'd said. He didn't have to be perfect to be with her.

"I love you, too," he said, leaning down and touching his lips to hers. He didn't get to kiss her as long as he would've liked, because the door to the suite opened again. He didn't let go of her though, when he looked to see who'd come in.

"Oh, good," Alissa said. "You two made up. Darcy."

The receptionist came forward, and she had two foot-longs in her hands. Gage started laughing, so glad when Sheryl joined in with him.

"Do you have time for lunch?" she asked, taking the hot dogs from Darcy.

"I think I can clear my schedule," Gage said.

Sheryl started for the door, but Alissa put her hand on Gage's arm. "You can bake, right?"

"Absolutely," he said. "But we should keep *her* as far from the kitchen as possible."

Alissa laughed, but Sheryl said, "I heard that," from the doorway.

Gage joined her with, "But I said it so quietly. How'd you hear that if I wasn't barking it?"

She shook her head, a smile on her face, and said, "Come on. I want to eat lunch with my boyfriend."

Gage reached over and picked up her tin foil wrapper before putting the last bite of his footlong in his mouth. This was his second one today, and it tasted amazing. The first he'd eaten in Sheryl's office with her, and that had been great too.

But South Port possessed something special, and he loved behind here with the woman he loved, eating the food he loved.

"How'd you know I'd be at that interview?" he asked, balling up their trash.

"Alissa called a family meeting last week," she said, her hand in his absolute perfection. "She wants to open a fish shop on Main Street. I guess she's rented a space and everything. She said she wanted to quit the head baker position."

"Ah," he said.

"I told her you were a great baker, and then I may have started...crying."

Gage's heart twisted in his chest. He didn't know what to say, so he pressed his lips to the top of her head. "My sisters and I are close," she said. "Even if I don't see them every day."

"That's nice. Michael left the island a week ago."

"I know. He texted me that I needed to go see you."

"He did?"

"Yeah, but that's the next story."

"Okay," he said with a chuckle.

"Anyway, Alissa put the job up, and you applied, and she texted me. We set everything up from there."

Gage let her words sink into his brain, and a rush of love for her filled him. She'd set everything up from there, because she loved him.

She loved *him.*

Britta barked, and Gage looked out at the ocean, the sight utterly beautiful. In the next moment, the dog took off, barking at the birds circling several yards away. Sheryl giggled in his arms, and Gage asked, "Michael texted you?"

"He said you were miserable," she said, tilting her head back to look at him. A teasing sparkle sat in her eyes.

"I wasn't *miserable*," he said, boldly lying right to her.

"I was," she said. "And I couldn't think of how to get you back. But then he texted, and you applied, and everything just came together." She kissed him, and Gage had never been happier in his whole life.

"And I think you were miserable," she whispered against his lips. "Just admit it." She traced her fingers through his hair and down the side of his face.

"Fine," he said, kissing her again. "I was miserable without you." And he'd never thought he'd ever need someone the way he needed Sheryl. But he did, and he was glad he did.

19

*S*heryl parked her new scooter about as close to the industrial door that led into the bottom level of the hotel as she could. She hung her helmet from the handlebars, because she didn't have fancy saddlebags like Gage.

One look to her left, and she found his motorcycle gleaming in the morning sunshine, though it was barely six o'clock in the morning.

He started work earlier now than he had while working the ferry, but he was much happier. Sheryl could see it in his face, hear it in his softer bark, and feel it in his touch. The man *loved* to bake, and he'd only been at Heartwood as the head baker for a couple of weeks, so he was still learning all the ropes.

But Sheryl could go upstairs to the bakery and find it fully stocked at this hour. They opened at six, so the cases would be full, and the line would be out the door. Gage didn't man the bakery, but he worked closely with Harriett, the baker manager, to make sure everything was stocked, ready, and fulfilled.

He got off at one in the afternoon now, and most days, Sheryl let him doze in her office while she finished her paperwork. Sometimes he simply went out to the beach and found a spot of sand to lie down on, and she'd find him lightly snoring while a family played several feet from him.

He wasn't working a second job, and they spent their afternoons napping and their evenings hand-in-hand on the beaches at South Port, or here at The Heartwood Inn. He'd worked security at a huge wedding here at the inn the last weekend before becoming the head baker, but Celeste kept asking him to take extra shifts for her events.

He'd declined them all, and while Sheryl knew her sister was irked, she couldn't get herself to care. Yes, she knew wedding crashing was a big deal, but Celeste could find her muscle somewhere else.

Sheryl entered her office and switched on the light. Sometimes she'd find a pastry sitting on her desk, a love note from Gage that didn't require any words. Today, her desk was empty, but that only reminded her that he was a man of mystery.

Her phone chimed, and Sheryl looked at it while she put her purse in the filing cabinet behind her desk. *The shop is open!* Alissa had sent. *Come get your fresh fish for dinner!*

A smile took up Sheryl's whole face. Alissa had wanted to be a fishmonger from the time she was five years old, and the dream had finally come true.

Dinner at the penthouse tonight, Olympia sent. *I'm with Gwen, and we just convinced Teagan to cook for all of us. SOs included.*

SOs.

Significant others. For once, Sheryl had one, and she wouldn't be attending a party as an odd-numbered wheel.

A sigh leaked from her lips as she sat down, happier than she'd been in a long time.

I do need a final count, Gwen said. *Within the next few minutes, as Teagan just left to get the fish.*

Numbers started flashing up on Sheryl's screen.

2 from Alissa. 2 from Olympia. She added her own 2, and then got her fingers flying to invite Gage to a fish fry with her sisters and their boyfriends. He wouldn't be able to answer right away, but she couldn't think of a reason why he wouldn't be in.

Gwen didn't answer, and Celeste was probably still in bed. She ran events that sometimes lasted well past midnight, and her office didn't open until ten.

Assume 2 for Celeste, Alissa said. *I heard she was seeing Boyd again.*

I thought it was Ben, Olympia sent.

At least it's not Andre, Sheryl tapped out and sent just

before Gwen said the exact same thing. She giggled at her phone, enjoying this sense of sisterhood though she was isolated on the bottom floor of this huge inn.

It's definitely not Ben, Alissa said.

Sheryl had just opened her laptop when another message came in. *It's not Ben, and it's six-freaking-AM!* Celeste had said. *I thought Grandma had fallen and broken another hip. Jeez.*

Just mute notifications, Olympia said, as if Celeste didn't know how to use her phone. Sheryl opted to stay out of that conversation, because she'd surely hear all about it tonight at dinner.

How many for you then? Gwen asked.

Put me down for two, Celeste said. *Since I'm up already.*

Who are you bringing? Alissa asked, and Sheryl could only assume the fish shop wasn't terribly busy if she had so much time to text.

I'll surprise you, Celeste said, and Sheryl rolled her eyes. Her sister definitely had a flair for the dramatic, and she'd probably show up solo. Which was fine. Teagan wasn't going to be angry about one wasted portion.

Sheryl got her notes together as the back door opened and shut again. Javier poked his head in and said, "Morning, Sher."

"How's the new baby?" she asked.

"Growing fast," he said, and she supposed it had been almost a month since the infant had been born.

"We'll come see him soon," she said.

"Okay." He lifted his hand in a wave as more people started gathering. She picked up her notes and went out to the common area where they held their morning meetings. She handed out assignments and then said, "I'm going to have a lemonade bar here tomorrow. Tell your wives and kids and friends. It'll be set up about nine and stay through the evening." She smiled around at her crew who worked so hard on the acres and acres of land the inn encompassed. "My sisters and I want to thank you for everything you do to make The Heartwood Inn the best it can be."

She didn't even care if Olympia approved the expense report for the lemonade bar. It was important that her employees knew they were valued, and if she had to pour the lemonade for twelve hours tomorrow, she would.

The meeting broke up, and Sheryl had reached the point in her new routine where she dashed upstairs to see Gage for a few minutes before she donned gloves and hitched a trailer to an ATV and got to work outside.

She grabbed her gloves from her office and took the stairs up to the first floor. Instead of going down the hall and into the lobby, she went outside and turned left toward the corner where the bakery waited for her.

The bell chimed when she entered, but she didn't see Gage. She was a little bit late, and he hadn't even answered her about the fish fry that night. Perhaps he was too busy for their fifteen minutes of breakfast.

She loved hot chocolate, no matter what the weather

was like, so she stepped up to the counter and ordered that, along with three ham and cheese croissants. Gage would eat two of them, and she'd nibble on the middle of hers where all the filling was. She'd rather conserve her calories for the liquid chocolate with whipped cream.

She'd sipped her treat while she waited for Gage, and she'd eaten her entire croissant by the time he bumped his way through the swinging black door behind the pastry cases. He looked to their table, his frustration evident. He stepped over to Harriett and spoke to her, taking his apron off and clapping his hands together before he came toward her.

"Hey." She rose to meet him, sensing something strange about him. "You okay?"

"Busy today," he said, sliding into the seat across the table from her, a smile filling his face. "It's so great to see you."

Sheryl ducked her head and giggled, definitely feeling like a teenager with her first serious boyfriend.

Six months later:

Sheryl could still ride her scooter to work, though the summer had ended. The tourists were gone, and the Christmas season had ended. She'd enjoy a few months with just locals on the island, and the groundskeeping slowed in the winter months. Thankfully.

She went in an hour later in the morning, and one day, she pushed into her office to find one of Gage's sweet treats sitting on her desk. From the glazed raspberries and strawberries with the immaculate swirls of whipped cream, she knew it was his lemon tart.

Her favorite.

Her mouth watered before she'd even sat down, and she didn't take the time to put her purse away before sitting down and picking up the plastic spoon he'd left for her. She made sure to get a bite of the pie crust, the custard, and a beautiful, red, ripe raspberry.

The tanginess from the custard and the sweetness from the fruit, along with the crunchy crust, made a party in her mouth. A groan started in her throat, and she closed her eyes and leaned her head back. "That is so good."

She put another bite in her mouth, put her purse away, and opened her laptop. She'd leant some of her crew to Celeste as one of the biggest weddings of the year was taking place next week, and she needed the extra manpower.

The door opened and closed, and her crew started to show up. She grabbed her folder of assignments for the day and put another bite of her tart in her mouth, intending to finish it after the meeting.

Something hard touched her tongue, and her first reaction was to spit out the dessert. She grabbed a napkin, surprise filing her, along with a bit of alarm. Her tongue separated the item from the custard, and she managed to get the object into the napkin.

She was aware of someone coming into her office, but she couldn't look away from the diamond ring staring back at her. "Oh, my word," she whispered.

"Oh, that's a good reaction," Gage said, and she jerked her attention up to him. He smiled down at her, pure love in his smile. "I love you, Sheryl." He took the napkin from her, because Sheryl's whole body had gone numb. Her brain didn't seem to be working.

Olympia had gotten engaged in October, but Alissa was still dating Shawn. Could Sheryl get engaged?

She and Gage had spent every day together for the past six months, and she loved him. She wanted to be his wife, and she wanted to have his babies.

He produced the newly-cleaned ring and got down on both knees. "Will you marry me?"

Excitement built beneath Sheryl's tongue, so when she said "Yes," it came out in a burst of air. She started laughing, and Gage swept her into his arms, also chuckling.

Sheryl's tears leaked out of her eyes as she cradled Gage's face and kissed him. "I love you," she said.

"I love you so much," he whispered back. "I can't wait to share my life with you."

Sheryl kissed him again, because she could only imagine the great adventures she and Gage would have together.

She'd never been happier, and she asked, "Will you make these lemon tarts for our wedding?"

"I'd do anything for you," he said, and Sheryl had never felt so loved.

Read on for a sneak peek at the next book in the series, THE HEARTWOOD WEDDING to meet another Heartwood sister!

SNEAK PEEK! THE HEARTWOOD WEDDING CHAPTER ONE

*B*radley Keith positioned the hardhat on his head, the construction site before him like a breath of fresh air. He loved the scent of concrete dust combined with the salty air only found on the island of Carter's Cove.

He'd been back in town for a few years now, and gratitude for this hometown project spread through him. Sometimes his jobs took him all over the South, and it was nice to have a construction site just down the road from where he lived.

The Heartwood Inn was the premier destination on the island, and they wanted another pool on the second floor for their VIP guests.

The floor was relatively quiet, as most of their conference center space sat on this floor, along with two huge ballrooms where the rich and famous booked their weddings. Brad knew, because his once-fiancée had booked their marriage-to-be right here at the inn. Thankfully, Emily had called off the wedding before Brad had had to do it.

"Where are we with the tiles?" he asked his floor supervisor.

James sighed. "They're delayed out of Atlanta. Apparently they've had some thunderstorms down there."

"Surprise, surprise," Brad muttered. He hated Atlanta, though he'd lived there for a few years. Started his construction business there, too. Maybe that was why he held such antagonistic feelings toward the city.

Because he'd almost lost everything there too, thanks to another fiancée that hadn't become his wife. And he had been the one to tell Tamara that the relationship wasn't going to work out between them.

That single act had caused him to lose his biggest financial backer—Tamara's father.

He wiped the memories from his mind as he surveyed what looked like one big hole in the cement. "Is she cured?"

"Yep," James said. "We just need those tiles. I have the guys working on the floor today. That'll be the second coat. We'll do the walls while we wait. And the floor tiles are in."

"They are? Show me those." Brad glanced at his clipboard as he followed James through the construction site.

A couple of men worked in the dressing rooms too, where the white subway tiles had gone in last week.

Brad felt like his whole life had been consumed by tiles. But when building an indoor swimming pool, that was kind of how things went.

"How was your date the other night?" James asked, stepping past a workbench filled with power tools.

"Oh, uh." Brad heaved another sigh. "I don't think I'm going to be seeing Carmen again." Anyone for that matter, but especially Carmen. He didn't date journalists, for one, and if he'd known who she was, he never would've agreed to go out with her. Number two, she hadn't really seemed interested in him, but in getting a story on him. And number three, she had the power to reduce him to ashes with a few strokes on her keyboard.

No, thank you. He'd left that high-profile life—but he hadn't been able to get out of the restaurant without a reason why he couldn't date her. He squirmed in his own skin just thinking about what he'd told her to get out of going on a second date with her.

"Why not?"

"I'm just not into the dating scene here," he said. "I grew up here, you know?"

"So? What does that have to do with anything?" James stopped in front of a stack of boxes. "These are the floor tiles for the pool surround."

Brad proceeded to cut through the tape on the top box to reveal—"These are red," he said.

"No." James frowned. "Didn't we order gray?"

"We sure did." Brad pulled one of the twelve-inch square tiles out of the box. "This is definitely red." He lifted the burnt orange tile almost above his head, wanting to smash it at his feet.

James made a sound like a leaking balloon, and he pulled his phone out of his back pocket. "I'll call them. Do you have the form?"

Brad did...somewhere. He looked at his clipboard and started flipping the papers attached there. "What was the name of the company again?" The letters in front of him blurred and rearranged themselves into nonsensical formations.

"Castle-something," James said.

A big C caught his attention, and he pulled that paper out of the top clasp. "I think this is it." No one knew about his reading struggles, and he'd managed to restart his business without help from anyone. Spending seventeen years playing professional football had allowed him certain...luxuries.

He'd returned to Carter's Cove, as there always seemed to be some sort of development going on here, and he'd managed to make a decent living the past few years.

"So you don't want to go out with Kelly," James said, looking at the paper.

"No," Brad said. "I'm not going out with anyone anymore." He'd been engaged twice, and he was thinking maybe he'd just stay married to his business, the way Tamara had claimed he already was.

Plus, at age forty-seven, he wasn't exactly in the prime years of his life for swimming in the dating pool. James had been the one to set him up with Emily here on the island, and in fact, every date Brad had been on once he'd re-established himself here in Carter's Cove had been set up by James.

"You could be missing out," James said, turning away a moment later with, "Yes, this is James Long with Keith Construction. We ordered...." His voice faded out, and Brad let him go.

He wandered out of the dressing room and back into the main pool area, where a few other people worked. He didn't have a huge construction firm, but he knew plenty of people, and when he got hired on a big job, he could bring the manpower.

He loved the beach, but he had a sudden longing to travel to Lexington, where he'd spent summers growing up on his grandfather's horse farm.

He'd lived a good life for his forty-seven years, even if he didn't have a wife and kids to show for it.

You might be missing out rang in his ears, but he scoffed them away. James didn't know what he was talking about. He couldn't even set Brad up with someone even remotely compatible with him, and they'd been friends for five years.

A feminine form moved past the plastic separating the

construction site from the rest of the hotel, and Brad turned away from the woman. Instant heat shot to his face, reminding him that even forty-seven-year-olds had hormones.

But Celeste Heartwood was one thousand percent off-limits. Not only was she completely out of his league, what with her pencil skirts and professionally pressed blouses—and those heels. Wow, Brad liked those heels that woman wore—but she knew she was out of his league.

"Did you hear me?"

"What?" Brad spun away from the plastic, where Celeste had been. She wasn't even there anymore, and foolishness hit Brad right between his ribs.

"They're putting a rush on the right tile," James said. "It should be here by the end of the week."

"Great," Brad said. "Great." He took a deep breath, wondering where he'd been on his to-do list for that morning before thoughts of Celeste had distracted him.

"Are you going down to South Port today?" James asked.

"Yes," Brad said, seizing onto the topic. "I do need to go down there."

"Okay, so—" He cut off so suddenly that Brad looked at him only to find him staring at something straight ahead. He followed his gaze to see Carmen Lunt standing there.

His stomach dropped to his boots, and whatever James

said didn't register in Brad's ears. All he could see was that fiery Latina stalking toward him. She said something in rapid Spanish that Brad knew enough to translate into something bad, and then she arrived in front of him.

"You said you were engaged?" The words echoed throughout the entire construction site, as it was mostly cement and very open.

"You said what?" James asked.

"I am," Brad said, his voice a little weaker than he'd like it to be.

"To who?" Carmen folded her arms and cocked one hip. Her head bobbled like one of those dolls, daring him to lie to her again.

He could see the headlines now…. He felt like he was falling for a moment, and his own name left his mind. Celeste walked by the plastic again, causing it to flutter, and he seized onto the idea. "Celeste Heartwood," he said. "There she is. Excuse me." He ducked around Carmen and jogged toward the plastic.

He'd known Celeste's family growing up, though he was quite a bit older than the woman herself. Olympia, her older sister, was probably five years younger than him, and Brad had competed in the surfing championship right here at the inn before he'd been drafted into professional football and shipped all over the country.

He'd spent the most time down in Florida, playing for the Falcons, where he'd ended his career after eight years there.

"Celeste," he called after her once he'd freed himself from the construction site. She turned back, surprise in those gorgeous eyes as she paused right outside her office door.

Gorgeous eyes? Where had that come from?

"Hey." He chuckled as he jogged up to her. "Can I talk to you? For a minute?" He glanced over his shoulder and back toward the construction site. James and Carmen hadn't emerged yet. She was his next-door neighbor, so maybe he was trying to calm her down.

Brad could hope and pray, and he needed a solution —fast.

"I suppose," Celeste said, confusion on her face.

"Great." He reached past her and twisted her door-knob, pushing the door in so she'd enter. Another quick look over his shoulder told him that he had maybe thirty seconds inside this office, as Carmen stood there, watching them now.

Celeste either didn't care or didn't see her, because she entered her office, one hand on the door while he followed. She closed the door and asked, "What's going on? Is there a problem with the construction? I can get the manager—"

"There's no problem with the construction." Brad pulled himself out of the situation and put himself on the football field. Sure, he'd retired from the league eight years ago, but he'd never focused better than when playing football.

And he needed to focus now, on the right things. Not Celeste's very feminine form, with all these curves and swells in the right place. Not her very pink lips that called to his male side. Not the pale blue eyes and the softly curled blonde hair that begged him to run his hands through it moments before he kissed her so completely that he'd forget the look of disdain on her face.

He really needed to get control of his thoughts, because he would never be with this woman.

"I said," she said. "What's the problem?"

"Oh, uh." He glanced behind him. "I need a favor, and I'm afraid I need it right now."

Carmen knocked on the door, a string of muffled Spanish following.

"What in the world?" Celeste asked, stepping one of those deliciously heeled feet toward the door.

Brad jumped in front of her. "I need you to say you're my fiancée."

Her eyes flew to his, wide and scared. Scared? Was that right?

Alarmed, for sure. Surprised. And yes, a little scared.

"Just tell her," he said. "Please, Celeste. It'll just be for the next ten minutes, and I just—" His voice got covered by louder knocking.

Pure desperation pulled through him, and he had no idea what he'd do if she said no.

She jumped as the door rattled in the frame as Carmen beat on it. She looked from it to him and tugged on the bottom of her blouse. It was pure white, with tiny pink palm trees on it, and Brad had a brief flash of the two of them lying on the sand, under some palm trees together.

"I'll take care of this," Celeste said, reaching for the door handle.

But that hadn't exactly answered Brad's plea, and he had no idea what she was going to say to the very angry woman on the other side of the door.

I can't wait to see what happens when Celeste opens that door! Get THE HEARTWOOD WEDDING in paperback, ebook, or audiobook today.

The Heartwood Sea (Book 1):
She owns The Heartwood Inn.
He needs the land the inn sits
on to impress his boss. Neither
one of them will give an inch.
But will they give each other
their hearts?

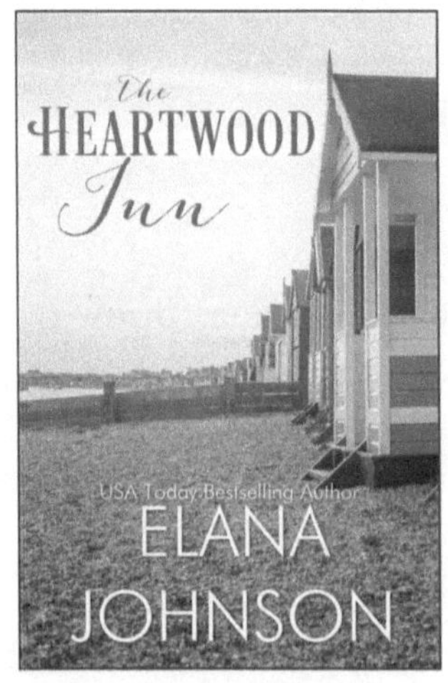

The Heartwood Inn (Book 2): She's excited to have a neighbor across the hall. He's got secrets he can never tell her. Will Olympia find a way to leave her past where it belongs so she can have a future with Chet?

The Heartwood Beach (Book 3): She's got a stalker. He's got a loud bark. Can Sheryl tame her bodyguard into a boyfriend?

The Heartwood Wedding (Book 4): He needs a reason not to go out with a journalist. She'd like a guaranteed date for the summer. They don't get along, so keeping Brad in the not-her-real-fiancé category should be easy for Celeste. Totally easy.

The Heartwood Chef (Book 5): They've been out before, and now they work in the same kitchen at The Heartwood Inn. Gwen isn't interested in getting anything filleted but fish, because Teagan's broken her heart before... Can Teagan and Gwen manage their professional relationship without letting feelings get in the way?

Overprotective Cowboy, Book 2: Can Ted and Emma face their pasts so they can truly be ready to step into the future together? Or will everything between them fall apart once the truth comes out?

Rugged Cowboy, Book 3: He's a cowboy mechanic with two kids and an ex-wife on the run. She connects better to horses than humans. Can Dallas and Jess find their way to each other at Hope Eternal Ranch?

Christmas Cowboy, Book 4: He needs to start a new story for his life. She's dealing with a lot of family issues. This Christmas, can Slate and Jill find solace in each other at Hope Eternal Ranch?

Wishful Cowboy, Book 5: He needs a place where he can thrive without his past haunting him. She's been waiting for the cowboy to return so she can confess her feelings. Can Luke and Hannah make their second chance into a forever love?

Risky Cowboy, Book 6: She's tired of making cheese and ice cream on her family's dairy farm, but when the cowboy hired to replace her turns out to be an ex-boyfriend, Clarissa suddenly isn't so sure about leaving town... Will Spencer risk it all to convince Clarissa to stay and give him a second chance?

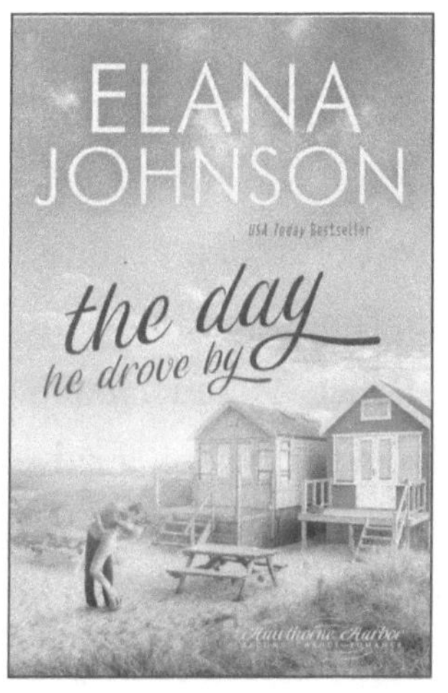

The Day He Drove By (Hawthorne Harbor Second Chance Romance, Book 1): A widowed florist, her ten-year-old daughter, and the paramedic who delivered the girl a decade earlier...

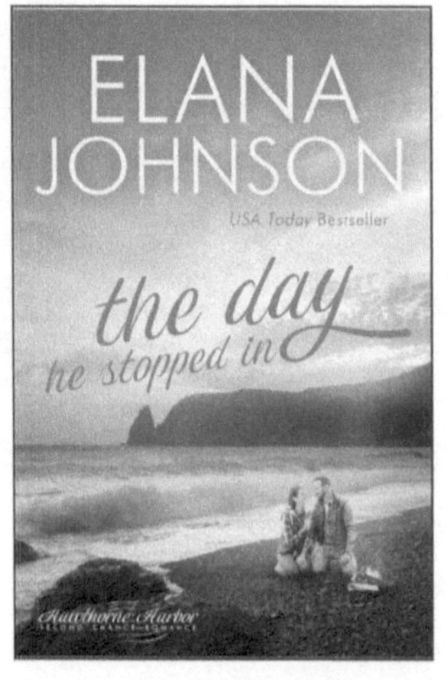

The Day He Stopped In (Hawthorne Harbor Second Chance Romance, Book 2): Janey Germaine is tired of entertaining tourists in Olympic National Park all day and trying to keep her twelve-year-old son occupied at night. When longtime friend and the Chief of Police, Adam Herrin, offers to take the boy on a ride-along one fall evening, Janey starts to see him in a different light. Do they have the courage to take their relationship out of the friend zone?

The Day He Said Hello (Hawthorne Harbor Second Chance Romance, Book 3): Bennett Patterson is content with his boring firefighting job and his big great dane...until he comes face-toface with his high school girlfriend, Jennie Zimmerman, who swore she'd never return to Hawthorne Harbor. Can they rekindle their old flame? Or will their opposite personalities keep them apart?

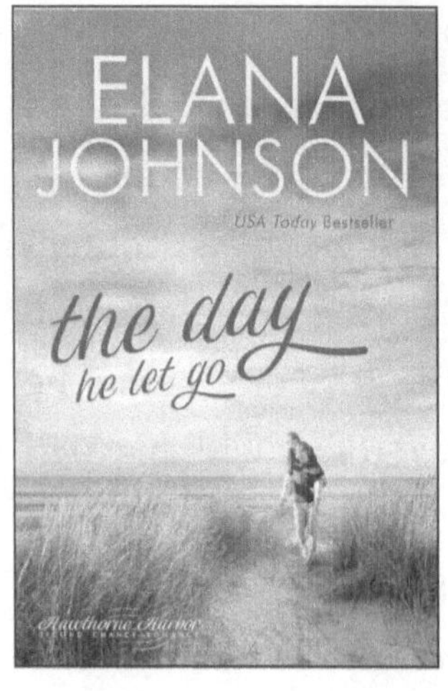

The Day He Let Go (Hawthorne Harbor Second Chance Romance, Book 4): Trent Baker is ready for another relationship, and he's hopeful he can find someone who wants him and to be a mother to his son. Lauren Michaels runs her own general contract company, and she's never thought she has a maternal bone in her body. But when she gets a second chance with the handsome K9 cop who blew her off when she first came to town, she can't say no... Can Trent and Lauren make their differences into strengths and build a family?

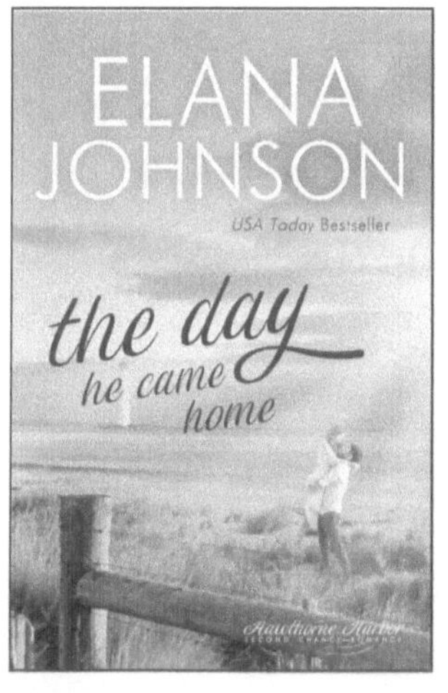

The Day He Came Home (Hawthorne Harbor Second Chance Romance, Book 5): A wounded Marine returns to Hawthorne Harbor years after the woman he was married to for exactly one week before she got an annulment...and then a baby nine months later. Can Hunter and Alice make a family out of past heartache?

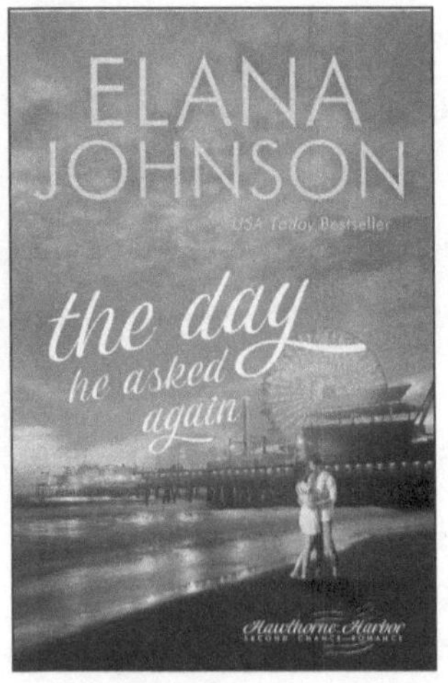

The Day He Asked Again (Hawthorne Harbor Second Chance Romance, Book 6): A Coast Guard captain would rather spend his time on the sea...unless he's with the woman he's been crushing on for months. Can Brooklynn and Dave make their second chance stick?

Getaway Bay (Book 2): Can Esther deal with dozens of business tasks, unhappy tourists, *and* the twists and turns in her new relationship?

Women's Beach Club (Book 3): With the help of her friends in the Beach Club, can Tawny solve the mystery, stay safe, and keep her man?

Straw and Diamonds (Book 4): Can Sasha maintain her sanity amidst their busy schedules, her issues with men like Jasper, and her desires to take her business to the next level?

The Billionaire Club (Book 5): Can Lexie keep her business affairs in the shadows while she brings her relationship out of them? Or will she have to confess everything to her new friends...and Jason?

Sweet Breeze Resort (Book 6): Can Gina manage her business across the sea and finish the remodel at Sweet Breeze, all while developing a meaningful relationship with Owen and his sons?

Rainforest Retreat (Book 7): As their paths continue to cross and Lawrence and Maizee spend more and more time together, will he find in her a retreat from all the family pressure? Can Maizee manage her relationship with her boss, or will she once again put her heart—and her job—on the line?

Getaway Bay Singles (Book 8): Can Katie bring him into her life, her daughter's life, and manage her business while he manages the app? Or will everything fall apart for a second time?

The Island Scandal (Book 2): Ashley Fox has known three things since age twelve: she was an excellent seamstress, what her wedding would look like, and that she'd never leave the island of Getaway Bay. Now, at age 35, she's been right about two of them, at least.

Can Burke and Ash find a way to navigate a romance when they've only ever been friends?

The Island Hideaway (Book 3): She's 37, single (except for the cat), and a synchronized swimmer looking to make some extra cash. Pathetic, right? She thinks so, and she's going to spend this summer housesitting a cliffside hideaway and coming up with a plan to turn her life around.

Can Noah and Zara fight their feelings for each other as easily as they trade jabs? Or will this summer shape up to be the one that provides the romance they've each always wanted?

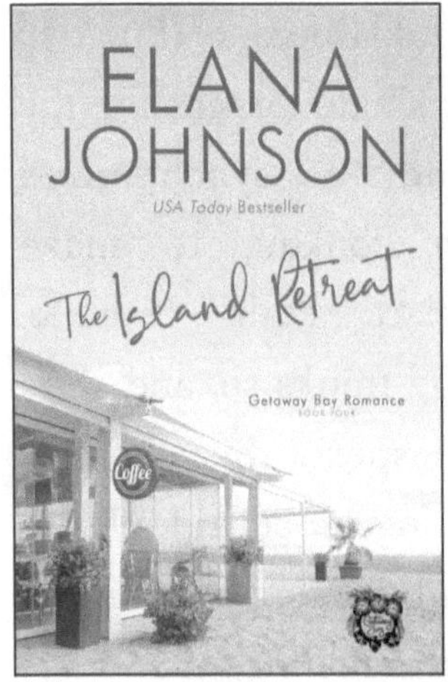

The Island Retreat (Book 4): Shannon's 35, divorced, and the highlight of her day is getting to the coffee shop before the morning rush. She tells herself that's fine, because she's got two cats and a past filled with emotional abuse. But she might be ready to heal so she can retreat into the arms of a man she's known for years...

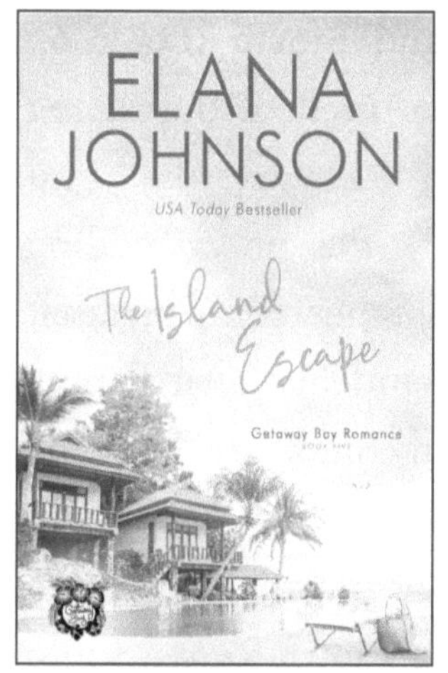

The Island Escape (Book 5): Riley Randall has spent eight years smiling at new brides, being excited for her friends as they find Mr. Right, and dating by a strict set of rules that she never breaks. But she might have to consider bending those rules ever so slightly if she wants an escape from the island...

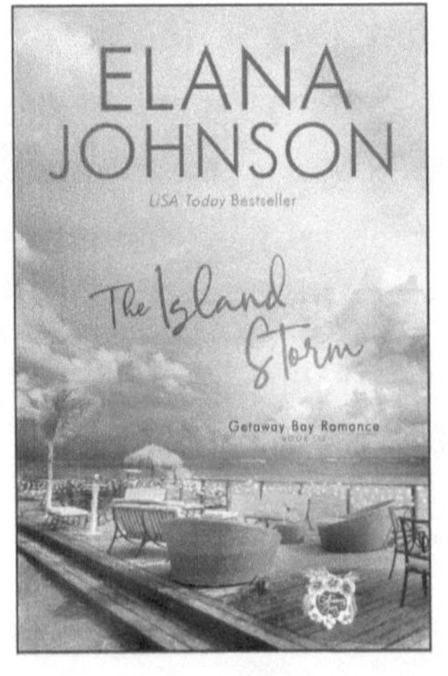

The Island Storm (Book 6): Lisa is 36, tired of the dating scene in Getaway Bay, and practically the only wedding planner at her company that hasn't found her own happy-ever-after. She's tried dating apps and blind dates...but could the company party put a man she's known for years into the spotlight?

The Island Wedding (Book 7): Deirdre is almost 40, estranged from her teenaged daughter, and determined not to feel sorry for herself. She does the best she can with the cards life has dealt her and she's dreaming of another island wedding...but it certainly can't happen with the widowed Chief of Police.

The Perfect Storm (Book 1): A freak storm has her sliding down the mountain...right into the arms of her ex. As Eden and Holden spend time out in the wilds of Hawaii trying to survive, their old flame is rekindled. But with secrets and old feelings in the way, will Holden be able to take all the broken pieces of his life and put them back together in a way that makes sense? Or will he lose his heart and the reputation of his company because of a single landslide?

The Overboard Mistake (Book 2): Friends who ditch her. A pod of killer whales. A limping cruise ship. All reasons Iris finds herself stranded on an deserted island with the handsome Navy SEAL...

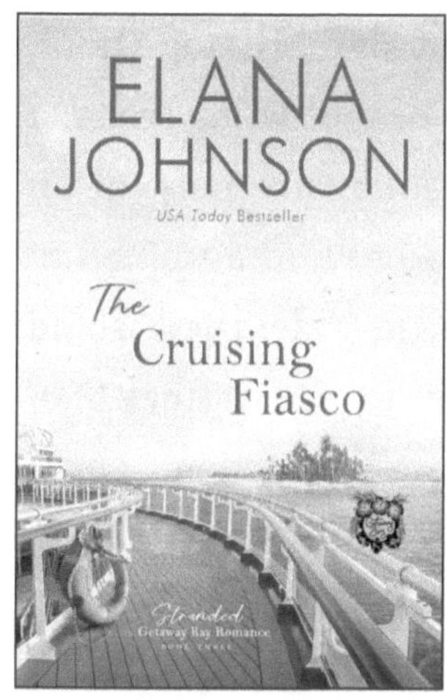

The Cruising Fiasco (Book 3):
He can throw a precision pass, but he's dead in the water in matters of the heart...

The Sand Bar Misstep (Book 4): Tired of the dating scene, a cowboy billionaire puts up an Internet ad to find a woman to come out to a deserted island with him to see if they can make a love connection...

ABOUT ELANA

Elana Johnson is the USA Today bestselling author of dozens of clean and wholesome contemporary romance novels. She lives in Utah, where she mothers two fur babies, taxis her daughter to theater several times a week, and eats a lot of Ferrero Rocher while writing. Find her on her website at feelgoodfictionbooks.com